JESSICA STEELE

no holds barred

Harlequin Books

TORONTO • NEW YORK • LONDON
AMSTERDAM • PARIS • SYDNEY • HAMBURG
STOCKHOLM • ATHENS • TOKYO • MILAN

Harlequin Presents first edition February 1985
ISBN 0-373-10766-8

Original hardcover edition published in 1984
by Mills & Boon Limited

CHAPTER ONE

LAINE inserted her key into the door of the semi-detached, and found the house unbearably quiet when she went in. She had just returned from seeing her parents off on their visit to New Zealand and Australia, and for the next three months quiet, she knew, was how it was going to be.

Walking into the sitting room, Laine dropped her shoulder bag down on to a chair and stared around the room. She saw nothing of the shabbiness of her comfortable home, its faded curtains and worn furniture, but saw only her home as it always had been; warm and loving.

The next three months were going to take some getting used to, she guessed, for there had always been laughter in the house. It had been a little quiet when her sister Nanette had married her New Zealander three years ago and had gone to the other side of the world; but shortly afterwards Tony had finished at university and the house was soon buzzing again with the multitude of friends he had gathered.

Reflecting for a moment on her brother's magnet-like, easygoing personality, Laine recalled that it had even come to the stage that, with his, 'Stay the night at my place—my parents won't mind,' they never knew who they would find sleeping on the settee when they came down in the morning.

Her eyes went to the settee, her thoughts going to Cristo, the newest and last of Tony's friends. Though Tony hadn't been around to discover more about the

Italian who had chosen to drown his sorrows in the same pub in which Tony had selected to have his farewell 'drink-in' on the eve of his departure for Australia.

Everyone in the pub that night had been included in the general convivial atmosphere. But Tony had kept sufficient awareness to realise that the young worse-for-wear foreigner, even if he had been able to remember the name of his hotel on this his first night in England, was in no condition to drive.

Her mother first down, had come across Cristoforo Forturini on the settee the next morning. 'Aspirin or bacon and eggs?' she had asked, not batting an eyelid to see their unexpected guest gaping as he sought for light in his alcohol-induced amnesia.

Her mind on that day, Laine recalled how cheerful her father had tried to be while Tony was there. But, Tony being his favourite, and so dear to him, they had been hard pressed at the airport to get a word out of Saul Balfour once Tony had gone through to the departure lounge. Both she and her mother had known that he was bleeding a little inside when he had insisted that they stay at the airport to wave Tony's plane off.

Perhaps initially, that was why Cristo had been made so welcome in their home. For the very next day he had returned bearing flowers for her and her mother, presenting them with a little speech in perfect English about his gratitude for giving hospitality to a lonely stranger in a foreign land.

'Stay and have dinner with us,' her father had promptly invited. And exchanging a glance with her mother, Laine had known that she too was thinking that behind her father's invitation was the hope that if his son was feeling a lonely stranger in the foreign land he had journeyed to, then some family might act similarly with his Tony.

After that, Cristo had become a regular visitor. And if at first he had been a shade on the solemn side for his twenty-five years, then her mother, used to young men of his age group, had soon had his smile coming more readioly. A firm friendship had developed between the two of them, and before long, learning that both mother and daughter were named Elaine, he was calling her mother the less formal 'Ella' by which she had always been known, and calling Laine by the name Tony had adopted, and everyone else since, when at the age of three he had acquired a sister, he had not been able to manage the two syllables of her name.

Deciding to have a cup of tea, Laine left the quiet sitting room, her thoughts back with her parents as she wondered where they were now.

Her mother had been dreadfully nervous about flying. But when Nanette had written a year ago to say that she was pregnant, and the idea had touched down that if they saved every penny they could, a journey to New Zealand might not be so impossible, so desperately had she wanted to see her first grandchild that the actual flying to get there had seemed the easy part.

There had been no thought in any of their minds then that Laine should not go with them. And she too had saved hard to make the trip. Then out of the blue, some seven or so months ago, Tony had announced that he was going to Australia to try his luck, adding, when he had seen how his father looked knocked for six, that all being well he would turn up in New Zealand while they were there.

Tony's decision to live in Australia had been a

terrible blow to her father, but the prospect of seeing him at Nanette's home had eased his pain a little, Laine had thought.

But only two weeks ago they had received a letter from Tony to say that he would not be able to make it to New Zealand. Never happier, he had written that he had met the most beautiful Australian girl who, to his astonishment, had agreed to marry him in a couple of months' time, and that any savings he had would be going towards their new home.

Cristo, Laine recalled, had been at their home when her father, putting in a little overtime at a job he liked but which did not pay very well, had come home and been handed the letter by her mother. He too had witnessed the way her father's eyes had lit up on seeing his son's handwriting, only for that glad light to fade as he read what Tony had penned. Saul Balfour had attempted to cover his floored feeling by showing pleasure that his son had found the wonderful girl he had written of, but none of them watching could mistake his despondency that no matter how hard he tried, there was just no way he could stretch his finances to make the journey to New Zealand *and* Australia.

Her mother had urged Cristo to stay to dinner that evening, with some hope, Laine rather thought, of lifting her father's spirits. But Cristo was by then more of a family friend than the stranger he had at first been, and before long her father had given up pretending that he was unaffected at having no idea now when he would, if ever, see his son again. When Laine had volunteered to do the washing up, Cristo, hamfisted in the kitchen, had as she had hoped straightaway offered to help. She had known then that he shared her opinion that by tactfully leaving her mother alone with her father, she might be the only one likely to help him over his dreadful disappointment.

'Your father will wish to see Tony married, I think,' suggested Cristo, taking hold of the tea-cloth as she handed him a washed up cup.

'It's out of the question, Cristo,' she had said quietly. But already her brain was busy.

That night in bed, Laine went to town on the gem of an idea that had come to her in the kitchen. Of course she would have to play her hand very carefully, for they did not come any prouder than her two parents. The next day, without telling anyone, she cancelled her flight.

It was for the sake of the mammoth pride of the two people she loved most in the world that, against all inclination, for the next seven days she accepted invitations to go out with Austin Culver. Austin too was one of Tony's many friends, though these days his frequent visits to their house had been more to try and get Laine to go out with him.

In truth, Laine thought Austin was a bit of a drag. But, as she turned her back on the unfairness she was practising by going out with him at all, to her mind— needs must when the devil drove.

Though three dates in quick succession with Austin were enough to have her declaring that she really must wash her hair when, smilingly, she turned down his fourth invitation.

'Tomorrow night, then?' he had pressed.

'I'd love to,' she had lied. 'Where shall we go?'

His face had cleared immediately. 'There's a motor-bike scramble . . .'

'Great,' she had replied, and wondered, if she wore a hat, if anyone would notice the ear muffs underneath.

So it was that, conscience pricking, she washed her hair which only that morning had seen the shampoo, and in consequence caused her mother to give her an old-fashioned look.

'You always were a fastidious child,' she stated, 'but *Austin Culver* is doing this to you!'

Wanting to burst out laughing at the very idea that she should want to be spruce day and night for the likes of Austin, Laine knew that her mother would smell a rat if, her sense of humour being very similar to her own, she let so much as a smile show through.

'I—like him, Mum,' she had answered quietly, hoping the way she had said it would convey that she more than liked him.

She saw her mother bite back some witty retort she had obviously thought better of making. Then, to save her from probably overplaying her hand by blurting out that she thought she was in love with him, the door bell went.

'I'll get it,' she said, and made her escape.

They had not seen Cristo for some days now. But Laine had been shaken, on opening the door, to see that he looked far from well.

'You should be in bed,' she admonished him sternly, leading the way into the sitting room, a flushed-cheeked Cristo following in her wake.

'I have been,' he replied. 'Only I had to come to say goodbye to all of you.'

'But we're not going until next week!' her mother had exclaimed, pushing him down into the chair he would most likely have collapsed into, by the look of him, if she hadn't.

'I know, Ella,' he had replied. 'It is I who am leaving.'

'*You're* leaving!' both she and her mother exclaimed, while her father inserted:

'I thought your brother had sent you to England for twelve months?'

'He never said precisely how long I should stay,' Cristo replied, choking on a cough. 'It was my assumption that I would be here for one year. But tonight I heard from my brother that I must go home immediately. Tomorrow—I leave.'

'But you're not fit to travel!' exclaimed Ella Balfour, her face showing her motherly concern for the flushed young man who had lost his own parents in a motor accident fifteen years ago.

'That is what I told Zare,' he smiled. And, trying to joke, 'I told him I thought I was dying.'

'But that didn't make any difference!' Laine exclaimed. Like her parents, she had grown fond of the young Italian who had been hard put to it to find a smile when they had first known him.

'He merely replied that if I was that ill, then that was all the more reason for me to return home promptly. It was his view that I should die in my native country.'

Callous brute! Laine thought, on her way to the late-opening chemist for the bottle of cough mixture her mother had sent her for; her father being sent upstairs for a thicker sweater than the one Cristo had on.

She knew all about Baldazare Forturini di Montonasco, even if Cristo had remained loyal to his brother when little by little he had revealed more and more about the head of the Forturini banking concern.

It was no wonder Cristo had been hard put to it to find a smile when he had first come to England. He had been forced by his brother, under the pretext of learning more about international banking, to leave Italy, but Zare Forturini's only object had been to get his brother away from the girl he had given his heart to. From what she had been able to glean, poor Cristo had fallen in love with a girl whom his brother had considered most unsuitable to bear the noble Forturini name.

Her heart had gone out to Cristo when, greatly unhappy, alone in a foreign land, he had told her of his love for Oriana.

'Why didn't you just marry her and stay in Italy?' she had asked, the solution, in her ignorance, simple to her. 'At twenty-five surely you don't have to have your brother's permission?'

'How would I afford a home?' he had replied. 'Apart from the fact that I would not like to go against my brother's wishes, I could not in any case inherit the fortune waiting for me without his consent.'

It was the first Laine had heard that there was a fortune waiting for him. And her mind went immediately to thinking that the cunning Baldazare Forturini would never consent to whoever Cristo wanted to marry. It was obvious to her then that his brother had designs in getting Cristo's money for himself.

In that, however, she was soon proved wrong, as tentatively she asked the question, 'You mean—if you don't marry—that you never come into your inheritance?'

'No, it is not like that,' Cristo replied, explaining, 'Like Zare, who has never found a woman suitable for his permanent taste, I can claim my inheritance when I am thirty-five.'

'Your brother has inherited his fortune?'

'He was thirty-five last year,' Cristo informed her.

And to tell her she had gone barking up entirely the wrong tree, 'As he is the elder, naturally his fortune is greater than mine.'

That Zare Forturini could not after all be trying to get his hands on her younger brother's inheritance did not make her feel any more kindly disposed to him as she hurried back with the cough mixture. And that he was a bachelor still was no surprise to her. For as she entered the sitting room she looked at Cristo being crooned over by her mother as he went off into a fit of coughing, and was of the opinion that, with or without his vast fortune, no girl in her right mind would find *him* suitable.

Poor Cristo, she thought as in the kitchen gratitude came that her mother had thought to stockpile a few provisions before she had left, he had been back in Italy for a week now. She did so hope the March weather of his own country had been able to do something toward clearing up his cough.

She opened a tin of baked beans, musing that if she didn't have any luck in her search for a temporary job tomorrow, her finances being what they were, her already slim figure would be positively skeletal by the time her parents returned, but when actions were halted by the ringing of the telephone.

Cowardice not to answer it touched down briefly. But her conscience struck about how she had deliberately used Austin Culver—and it was bound to be him—and she went to pick up the instrument.

'Did they get off all right?' asked Austin after an enthusiastic greeting that told her it wasn't going to be as easy to put him down as it had been to pick him up.

'Yes, thanks,' she answered, aware she had nothing in common with him, but guilt having her searching for something else to say. 'The plane took off exactly on time.'

'A pity your employers changed their minds about letting you have the time off at the last minute,' said Austin. And to make her cringe, 'Though from my point of view, I can't be sorry you couldn't go.'

Oh help, Laine thought, realising she had landed herself with an undiluted diet of his company for the next three months—if she couldn't do something about it.

'Yes—it was a shame,' she said, ignoring his latter remark, feeling safer discussing the way her dastardly boss, who was in truth one of the nicest men she knew, had told her at the last minute that he had found it impossible to get the right sort of temporary replacement for her. But neither Austin, nor anyone else who might tell her family, must be allowed to guess that only yesterday Mr Paterson had shaken her warmly by the hand, wished her 'Bon voyage', and told her to hurry back. 'But then Mr Paterson did only half promise at the outset that I could have the time off,' she said, trying to ease the guilt that was piling up on her at the whoppers she had told.

'Did your father get in touch with him?' Austin asked. 'He said he was going to when I was talking to him the night you came home and said you couldn't go.'

'It wouldn't have done any good,' Laine replied, recalling how she had broken out into a cold sweat at her father's suggestion that he would ring Mr Paterson in the morning.

'No, I don't expect it would,' said Austin. And with a broad hint, 'I expect you're lonely now that your folks have gone.'

'Oh, I haven't had time to feel lonely yet,' said Laine quickly, barely pausing to draw another breath before she was telling him, and forestalling what she guessed was coming—a suggestion that he came round to keep her company. 'I'm feeling rather whacked, actually—it's been an eventful day. I'm going to have an early night.'

'Oh,' disappointment was in his voice, then, 'I'll give you a ring tomorrow, then, shall I?'

'If you'd like to,' said Laine. And getting hot under the collar as a sudden terrible thought occurred to her, 'Only don't ring me at work, will you. They—er—don't like us to have personal calls.'

'Who's to know?' he came back. 'With you on the switchboard . . .'

'All calls have to be logged,' she put in quickly, inventing, 'incoming as well as outgoing calls.'

'You're that honest!' he exclaimed.

If only he knew, Laine thought. 'I like to do my job efficiently,' she replied.

Breathing a sigh of relief that she would not be hearing from Austin again for another twenty-four hours, Laine put down the phone, squirming a little about her blatant dishonesty in recent events as she went back to her baked beans.

Not that she could regret any of what she had done. It was worth it to see her father rapidly perk up when, after a tussle, he had been persuaded that if only he would lower his pride, the means were now at his disposal for him and her mother to attend Tony's wedding. Even if it meant that it might be years before she saw Nanette and the baby, seeing the happiness shining in her father's eyes as he had sworn to start saving the minute he got back to repay her, Laine could not regret it.

She'd had to go carefully, of course. Her mother, for one thing, was as sharp as a tack. And for a start, she had had to knock all idea from her father's head of ringing her boss. Austin had come in very useful then. Though of course she had had to wait until he had gone home that night before, a little hesitantly it had to be admitted, she had told both her parents:

'Actually, Dad—Mum, I—er—wouldn't mind too much—just at the moment—if I didn't—er—come with you to New Zealand.'

Her hesitancy had been no act. Even if all her lies were for a good cause, she didn't find it very easy to lie to them.

'Not mind!' Saul Balfour had echoed, startled. 'But you've been looking forward to . . .'

'I know,' she'd said quickly, and had fought then to get the lie out unblushing. 'But—well, Austin . . .'

Her father had caught on then. Her hesitancy was working in her favour, it appeared, and he thought she was a little embarrassed to be telling them that having started to date Austin, she was beginning to form an attachment for him.

'My little girl,' he had said, gently teasing. 'You don't want to leave him—is that it?' while her mother, who knew her better than anyone, looked slightly askance, and exclaimed:

'Austin Culver!'

Laine had thought her mother was going to be the more sticky proposition of the two. But maybe because the time of her maiden flight was drawing near, nerves were attacking whenever she thought about it, or maybe because when she wasn't worrying about flying the rest of her time was eaten up with the anticipation of seeing her new granddaughter, after her disbelieving look that her youngest child seemed to be romantically inclined to the last man she would have thought of her falling in love with, she had nothing more to say.

In the event, her father did not telephone her boss.

And as time went on, Laine knew she could not delay any longer in getting her father to see that since she now no longer had any use for her savings, he might as well have her money.

Having spent most of the day rehearsing what she had to say, Laine was more than pleased when during their meal that night, the visit to New Zealand again under discussion, she had pushed back a wing of blonde hair from her forehead, and had brought out, as though she had only just thought of it:

'Hey, what's the matter with you and Mum taking my money to get you to Tony's wedding?'

Her baked beans on toast demolished without her having any recollection of eating them, Laine took her used utensils to the sink and washed them up, reflecting on the tussle that had gone on until nearly bedtime. But she had gone to bed happy, because by then, at long last, her father's longing to see Tony had seen him able to swallow his pride under her persuasion that she was family after all, and that many was the time in the past that she had borrowed from him.

Now, she mused, thinking she might well have an early night after all, she had only two problems. How on earth was she going to let Austin down gently? It just didn't seem right, even if he was unaware of just how useful he had been, to abruptly drop him now that his usefulness was at an end. Her other problem was that of finding a job to tide her over until the temp who had taken over her job departed in three months' time.

That she didn't have a job to go to had been something of a shock to her, Laine admitted as she went and got ready for bed. It had been in her mind to ring up Mr Paterson tomorrow and tell him that her plans had changed and that she did not need three months off after all.

But the day before yesterday, having, she owned, too many other things on her mind to give much thought to what Luckman's were going to do without a telephonist for three months, she had been introduced to the young woman who had been brought in so that she could show her the ropes.

And having met Rosalie Denton, learning more and more about her sad circumstances in the odd lull here and there, there was no way she could deprive the young widow of the salary she had already spent on paper for new clothing for her two young children.

Something will turn up, Laine thought as she got into bed, hoping she wouldn't have the same difficulty Rosalie had told her she had experienced in finding a short-term job to give her a financial breathing space.

Laine had just settled her head on her pillows, thinking that she didn't mind what sort of a job she did, that perhaps a change from being the telephonist at Luckman's might do her good, when the instrument she thought she was having a rest from rang.

Dratting, if it was Austin Culver again, that the telephone had ever been invented, Laine pushed back the covers and got out of bed.

She was, she owned, feeling very slightly niggled as she picked up the receiver, and her clear speaking voice, always slightly husky, part of the reason she had been taken out of the post room and trained for Luckman's switchboard, had a touch of irritation to it as she gave her number.

'Elaine Balfour?' queried a voice that definitely was not Austin's or, from the merest trace of a foreign accent, any other Englishman either.

'Speaking,' she replied, her husky tones mellowing a

little as her interest was aroused. Though not for long, for her caller was waiting no longer than to have confirmation that he had the right party, before, those tones hardening, just as though he was used to bossing people around, she heard him say:

'You will be so good, *signorina*, as to transport yourself to Italy immediately.'

Her first thought then was that it was Cristo playing some game with her—though never had she heard Cristo sounding so authoritarian—and besides, Cristo's voice had nothing of the biting quality that this voice had.

'Who, may I ask, have I the pleasure of speaking with?' she replied at last, sarcasm coming as she rejected any vague notion that one of Tony's mad friends were playing silly devils.

But it was not a game, she very soon learned. And her caller had not been made any pleasanter by her sarcasm. Though she very nearly dropped when tersely his voice came again, as he informed her:

'My name is Baldazare Forturini.' And while she was still blinking that she was actually speaking to Cristo's cruelly unsympathetic brother, he was going on to command, 'You will take the first flight possible,' astonishing her that he thought he could calmly order her to Italy in the same way he had ordered Cristo back, when at the time Cristo had been far from well.

'Who the *dickens* do you think you are?' she was questioning then, and with some heat. And, not giving him time to tell her, she rushed in to tell him, 'You may have your brother jumping to obey your "Come when I call" bidding, *signore*, but don't you dare think for one minute that you can boss me . . .'

She had broken off, the heat leaving her as common

sense came to question that even a man as autocratic as
Baldazare Forturini wouldn't think he could give his
orders to someone he had never met, unless he had
good reason to think he would not meet up with any
opposition. Or would he? There was only one way to
find out.

'Why should I go anywhere?' she questioned shortly,
her voice growing snappy again lest he thought she was
in any way giving in to him. 'You have no right . . .'

'I have every right,' he clipped, causing her anger to
soar that he wasn't allowing her to finish. 'My brother
Cristoforo is ill, gravely ill.'

'And whose fault is that?' she flew back at him, too
incensed by what she knew of him for that word
'gravely' to register properly. 'If you hadn't been so
dogmatic in insisting, when you knew he wasn't well,
that it would be better for him to die in his own
country . . .' Suddenly, the word 'die' had the word
'gravely' at last registering, and her anger disappeared
without trace. 'Gravely ill?' she queried huskily. 'You
said Cristo is—gravely ill?'

'The crisis is near,' he told her, no emotion in his
voice to give her a clue as to how Cristo's condition
was affecting him. But he was succeeding in
astonishing her again, when, his voice level, he told
her, 'My brother is calling for you.'

'He's calling for—*me*?' she just had to question,
sadness taking her in its grip even while she was
thinking that if Cristo was calling for anyone, she
would have thought it would be Oriana, the girl he
had been in love with, and probably still was in love
with as far as she knew.

'You are wasting time.' That hard note was back
again she heard. 'Do as I say,' he was back to ordering.
'Take the next plane. You will . . .'

'I—can't,' Laine broke in, her heartstrings being torn, no anger in her now at being ordered about by him.

But her pride was to be stirred when thundering back to singe her ears came the words, nothing the matter with his familiarity with a language that was not his own either, 'You heartless bitch!' And it was that pride that had her getting in there quickly before he could add another insult, her tones gone to be aloof:

'Not so much heartless, *signore*,' that aloofness needed for pride's sake as she was forced to tell him, 'More penniless than heartless, I assure you.'

She hadn't expected to be able to keep his insults at bay for long. But to hear an explosion in Italian, before he had sufficient control to slam into her in a language she did understand had aloof pride sent on its way. '*Dio!*' he roared, 'that any woman should want paying to visit a hospital where . . .'

'Paying?' she exclaimed, anger flaring as she rushed on. 'It's not that I want payment at all. I . . .'

'Like hell you don't,' he refused to hear her out. 'I have full proof that you have been amply rewarded for your—favours.'

It was Laine's turn to explode. 'What the hell do you mean by that?' she blazed. 'I've never taken so much as a penny from . . .'

'On top of everything else, do not call my brother a liar,' she was chopped off arrogantly. And before she could fly in again, Baldazare Forturini went on to try to flatten her by gritting, 'I still hold the letter in which he requests I advance him two thousand English pounds so that he can make you a gift for your many *kindnesses*.'

'Kindnesses!' gasped Laine, latching on to the last stressed word, though none of it made very much

sense. But she only earned some more of his wrath as,
tautly, he said:-

'An old-fashioned term for what you and my
brother got up to, wouldn't you say?'

Staggered at his nerve, Laine got as far as, 'How
dare . . .' before again she was bluntly chopped off.

'I dare,' he grated, 'because unlike you, I have never
been ashamed of the truth.' And having given her that
to chew on, aggression in every syllable, Zare
Forturini showed her just how unashamed of the truth
he was by telling her, 'It is precisely because I could
see that Cristoforo had been softheaded enough to fall
for a self-centred apology for a woman who would take
him for every penny—if I allowed it—that I recalled
him with all speed to his homeland.'

Reeling at the thought that, by the sound of it, she,
Laine Balfour, was the reason for Cristo being so
promptly ordered back to Italy, Laine saw that she
could argue until she was blue in the face and his
overbearing brother would never believe her.

'And you were obeyed, weren't you?' she replied
snappily. 'That he was ill made no difference to you.
You . . .'

'I thought any risk was worth taking to get him
away from the likes of you,' burned her ears.

'Well, I hope you're satisfied,' she flared. 'You
certainly got your wish in getting him away from the
likes of me—more than one wish,' she raced on, more
anger coming as what he had said sank in deeper. 'You
not only have Cristo away from my sort. But, if *you*
are to be believed, your brother may well die in his
own country.'

Who slammed the phone down first, Laine had no
way of knowing. Though she was fairly certain, as
some foul Italian epithet rocketed down the line, foul

she was sure even if she didn't comprehend it, that his receiver had been banged down too. But, stunned, for long moments she just stared at the instrument, the tingling of her blood still there to tell her that she had not just dreamed the whole thing.

Minutes later, that certain sensitivity in Laine was having her appalled by her parting remark to Cristo's brother. Surely he must love Cristo very much, or why else would he so summarily summon him home when he thought some fortune-hunter had got her claws into him? He must love him very dearly, she saw, otherwise he would never have telephoned her to try and get her to go to Italy.

That, when Zare Forturini loved his brother, she had rubbed it in that it was his wish that his brother should die in his own country, gave Laine long moments of anguish in wishing that she had not said it.

It was no excuse to tell herself that having no liking for what she had heard of him—and had been able to fill in for herself—before his phone call, that his authoritarian way of speaking to her, or his lashing out at her, had made him any more endearing.

But she was not made to feel any better as she wondered why on earth Cristo had told him he wanted to give her a present of two thousand pounds! For all Zare Forturini, with his abhorrence of lies, believed that Cristo had not lied to him when telling him what he had wanted the money for, it was plain that Cristo had done exactly that. They were a moneyed family, were the Forturinis, but even so, until Cristo was able to inherit his own fortune, it looked very much as though he was being made to exist on the money he earned. Laine guessed then that Cristo must have found living in England expensive. Most likely he had run up a few bills and, where two thousand to her was a whacking sum, Cristo must have let his debts pile up without thinking about them too much, but had not wanted to confess that he had overspent when asking his brother for an advance.

Laine returned to her bed with her spirits at a very low ebb. Everything in her was saying that if Cristo was so ill, then she ought to be rushing to his bedside. Yet how could she go? She had given her parents all she could lay her hands on, there just wasn't any way she could scrape up her air fare to go to him.

Tossing and turning as she tried to get to sleep, she tried to convince herself that it would make no difference to Cristo's chances of recovery that she was not there. In his delirium, she fretted, Cristo could have called out for anybody. Driven by whatever gremlins were in his head as he fought his way through the crisis, it did not necessarily mean that the person he called out for was the person he wanted to see.

Laine had little sleep that night as in turns she worried and prayed for Cristo. But as dawn broke, every conceivable and inconceivable notion gone through of how she could scrape together enough to get her to Italy, she finally laid the matter to rest when her head cleared a little and she realised that even if she could find the wherewithal—and on the face of it that looked impossible—there would be little point in making the flight. For apart from knowing that Cristo had his home with his brother in a rural area in Tuscany, she had no further idea of his address.

CHAPTER TWO

MARCH had given way to April when, in the early evening of that Sunday, Laine, stretched out on the settee and started counting the days to her parents' return.

They had been away a month now, and while she wanted nothing more than that they should enjoy every minute of their holiday, with her worries piling one up on top of the other, she would not have minded seeing her father walk in through the door, and hear him ask, as occasionally he had in the past, 'Now, what's your problem?'

Protected, as now she recognised she always had been by her family—not surprising, she supposed, since she was its youngest member—she was finding it hard that, for the first time in her life living alone, she had no one there to turn to when her problems started to get out of hand.

Rosalie Denton had not been joking, she had found, when she had told her that temporary jobs were almost impossible to get. For the only work Laine had so far been able to find had been a week's work which had ended yesterday, in a poorly paid job as a run-about cake shop assistant.

So much for her optimistic 'something was bound to turn up' thoughts of a month ago, she thought glumly, and the memory of the sparse contents of her purse did not make her feel any brighter.

Thank the lord she'd been able to get out of going to yet *another* motor-bike scramble with Austin today, she reflected, seeking to find alternative thoughts from those on her impecunious state. Austin was becoming a positive pain. Yet because of the guilt she felt at the way she had so unashamedly used him, she had not so far been able to find it in her to say 'Goodbye' to him.

And what with Austin, her desperate need to find some temporary work, and the constant nagging in her mind of whether poor dear Cristo had made it through his crisis, Laine owned that she was not a little fed up.

Deciding to have a bath and an early night when, with luck, things might look better in the morning, Laine left the settee. The only bright spot, she considered as she ran her bath, was those happy letters she received from her parents. Her mother was little short of ecstatic about the baby. Never, Laine realised, had there ever been a baby such as this one. Page after page had been written about her beautiful niece, so that after one glowing report, Laine had actually found herself wishing that she was in New Zealand herself to see and to hold for herself this little marvel of nature.

Not that she could ever regret her decision not to go, she thought, as she stepped into her bath. The postscript her father had added to her mother's last letter, the joy that had come across that soon they would be in Australia actually attending Tony's wedding, was all she needed to know that she had been right to do what she had.

Her mind flitted to the postscript her mother had tacked on after seeing her father's reference to Tony's wedding. 'Can we expect to hear wedding bells for you and Austin when we return?' She hoped her mother was joking.

She would have to use a load of tact when answering that letter, she mused, just in case her mother hadn't been joking. Perhaps it would be better if she didn't mention Austin at all. Perhaps then her parents might start to get the idea that he was not so important in her life after all.

Soaping herself, Laine recalled other letters she had written to her parents. Other letters in which another person had not been referred to.

Cristo was back in her mind as he often was since that snarling phone call from his odious brother. She had deliberately not told her parents about that phone call either, or that barked accusation that Cristo had given her two thousand pounds. For how could she?

To tell her parents anything about it would mean having to tell them how ill Cristo had been. And with her mother taking Cristo to her heart and acting like a mother to him too, she would be dreadfully upset not knowing whether he had survived his illness. Nothing, Laine decided, should be allowed to mar this holiday that had so been looked forward to.

The bath water going cold, she ran in more hot. And with no particular urgency to do anything, she lay back, thinking again, as she had often done, of that phone call from that ghastly Baldazare Forturini.

He sounded just as awful as she had always thought him. Thank goodness she had never met him. He had been over to England on business a couple of times while Cristo had been here. But, busy as Cristo had said his brother always was, he had found time to see him, though, for small mercies be grateful, Cristo had never brought him to meet the family with whom he spent so much of his spare time.

Her bath water was growing cold again as Laine's thoughts became a mixture of the bane of her life Austin Culver, sadness for Cristo, and a hearty dislike for his brother, and to thinking again that her mother could not possibly have been serious with her suggestion that there might be the sound of wedding bells for her soon. When the notion came to her suddenly to wonder if there was something wrong with her that, so far, she had not met any man she fancied enough to marry, Laine left her bath.

Perhaps her mother had made her home too comfortable for her, she pondered as, catching a glimpse of herself in the bathroom mirror, she stayed to study her wide deep blue eyes, her clear skin and tendrils of damp blonde hair that clung to her unlined forehead.

Or maybe it was that, having seen a whole army of Tony's friends tramp through the house, some of them unshaven and very unprepossesing when viewed in first light sleeping on the settee, she could not get romantically enthusiastic about men in general.

Wrapped in a towelling robe while she went into her bedroom to unearth a fresh nightdress, the thought came that at twenty-two life should be more exciting than it actually was. She had just extracted a clean nightdress from her chest of drawers when the front door bell went.

Oh God, was her initial groaning reaction, had the motor-bike scramble finished already? That it was only just dusk told her that Austin must have galloped all the way to get there so soon on the offchance that she would invite him in.

He can jolly well wait, she thought crossly when the bell pealed again, guilt in her conscience not as strong as it had been when she had thought of him miles away; that guilt diluted by knowing that he was actually on her doorstep.

As she was about to get dressed, the door bell

pealed for a third time, and she had second thoughts. Perhaps if she went to the door as she was, Austin might see that she meant it when she said she was having an early night. Maybe that would convince him that he stood no chance of coming in for a cup of coffee and a chat.

Tightening the belt of her pale pink robe, guilt returning to pin a smile she didn't feel on her face, Laine tripped lightly down the stairs just as the bell rang for an imperious fourth time.

But the shape that met her gaze as she opened the door was not the leather-gear-clad gangling Austin at all! Even as her smile fell away as her eyes registered a tall, dark-haired, dark-eyed expensively-suited man standing there, no smile about his firm-lipped mouth either, Laine recognised that if he tried from now to next year, Austin would never ever look like this sophisticated-looking man.

Feeling oddly threatened as the dark stranger scowled and unspeakingly let his eyes sweep from the top of her fair head and scrubbed face to the tips of her bare feet, Laine found she had to struggle to find her voice, when he did not appear in any hurry to tell her what he wanted.

'Yes?' she questioned, her voice husky as it normally was, but more so now as that sensation of feeling threatened caught her by the throat. 'You—were ringing the bell,' she added, inanely she thought, since he knew that. But nerves were attacking as she took in more of his aristocratic patrician features, the unbidden thought coming that he would be really something if he allowed that bronze-skinned face to crack in a smile.

What she had expected him to answer, she wasn't sure. Maybe that he wanted directions somewhere, she speculated, for everything about him shouted that suburbia was not his usual habitat. But what he did say had her eyes shooting wide, as in very slightly accented tones, that scowl still there, he said:

'Your voice is beautiful,' his eyes steady now on her face, 'as is the rest of you.' And while that trace of accent was registering, Italian if she wasn't mistaken, he was completing what her natural intelligence was trying to tell her, by adding uncivilly, 'It is a pity that my brother did not look beneath the surface of you to your hard self-centred heart before he became infatuated with you.'

The name Baldazare Forturini was all that had time to light down, before her anxieties for Cristo this past month forced his name from her lips.

'Cristo!' she said chokily, half in exclamation, half in a question to know what fate had befallen him.

But no answer was forthcoming, just more of the plentiful supply of aggression she saw Baldazare Forturini had at his command. For it was sharply that he charged:

'You do not deny that my brother is infatuated with you?'

Taking heart from the present tense of the '*is* infatuated with you' he had used, Laine was in no mind to answer his questions either.

'How is he?' she asked quickly, needing urgently to know that the young man who had warmed the hearts of all of them in the seven months of their knowing him was well. But fear was touching her again when all she received for her trouble was a hard stare. 'He— Cristo—he d-did get better, didn't he?'

For her pains, Laine was on the receiving end of more aggression as, 'Dio!' he snarled. 'You *dare* to *pretend* that you care?'

'Of course I care!' Anger was stirring in her. But she got no further than flaring, 'I . . .' before she was cut off, as, his chin jutting, that dark Italian barked:

'You care only because if he is dead then you know that your money supply has died with him!'

Recovering from that, a second later her anger would have gone soaring. But suddenly she was seeing a reason for this arrogant man's aggression. And her voice had gone choky again, when with no more than a whisper, she asked fearfully:

'He's—he's not—dead, is he?'

Fearing the very worst, all she received for an answer was Baldazare Forturini's steady stare. But it was in that moment of high tension, while his eyes were taking in her every feature, that Laine suddenly came to to realise that whatever it was this hard-eyed Italian had come to tell her, the doorstep was not the place for him to tell her of anything that concerned anything terrible about Cristo.

'You—had better come in,' she invited reluctantly, that sense of feeling threatened coming over her again as he followed her into the worn but comfortable sitting room.

His eyes going over her figure, curving and feminine still despite the shapeless garment covering her, made her feel edgy as she invited him to sit down. She did not have a stitch on beneath her robe, and she knew as his eyes flicked to the valley at the vee of her covering that, worldly-wise, he knew that.

'I'll go and put some clothes on,' she murmured, pulling her robe closer about her. 'I wasn't—expecting visitors.'

'Do not bother on my account,' he replied coldly, his look sceptical at her statement that she wasn't expecting ary visitor as he declined her offer to be seated.

Since it did not look as though he would stay above two minutes, Laine changed her mind about going to get dressed, hoping the sooner to learn that Cristo was alive and well—she just could not believe that the so alive young man could be dead.

But, expecting that when next Baldazare Forturini opened his mouth, it would be to tell her about Cristo, she was again seeing how she could expect only the unexpected from the aristocratic-looking Italian. For he was not, she heard, going to tell her anything of what she wanted to know until he was good and ready.

'You live here alone?' he asked, his eyes leaving her to do a quick survey of the room.

It became obvious to her then that Cristo could have told him nothing about her family. Had he done so, this man who was now looking as though he thought it wouldn't have hurt her to part with some of that two thousand she was supposed to have received on some new curtains would have known that she normally lived with her parents. But she'd be damned if she would apologise for her home.

'At the moment, yes,' she told him stiffly.

The small movement of his right eyebrow ascending was all she needed to know that nothing she wanted to hear would soon be coming her way.

'You are saying there has been no time for you to install someone new since Cristoforo moved out?' he asked insultingly. And his eyes going to her towelling-covered breasts, 'With your charms, *signorina*, surely not?'

Only by a short margin did Laine manage to keep her temper. 'For your information, *signore*,' she told him tartly, 'your brother did not live here.'

Her sharp reply was considered for one moment,

but he was not, she discovered, backing one iota away from what he had made up his mind was going on between her and his brother.

'Maybe he did not spend every evening with his head on your pillow,' he conceded, 'but, from the little he has told me, I know that it was with you he spent most of his spare time.'

Laine could not deny that. Though it was more with the Balfours as a family he had spent his non-working hours. But never had there been anything of what Baldazare Forturini was suggesting between her and Cristo. For at the start, Cristo had been too lovesick for his Oriana to so much as notice any other woman. And by the time his pain had eased, Laine had discovered that, given he was a foreigner, he was no different from any of Tony's other friends.

About to argue that the relationship between her and Cristo was more like that of brother and sister than anything else, Laine suddenly brought herself up short. Wonder was taking her that such was Baldazare Forturini's manner, having angered and frustrated her both at the same time, astonishingly she had let him indulge in a welter of insults without finding out the answer to the only reason she had invited him in in the first place.

'I'm not in the witness box,' she said to let him know that she was not going to answer any of his charges. But her voice began to weaken when she went on, 'So will you kindly tell me what has—happened to Cristo? How—he is?'

Dark eyes surveyed her as the man she now recognised as an opponent took time to let his glance travel to where her blonde hair curved under at the fine line of her jawbone. Then with his eyes fixed on the dark blue of hers, finally he deigned to tell her:

'His life hung on a very thin thread for a while. But he is now out of hospital.'

Just like a bubble that had been pricked, so as he finished speaking, every scrap of anger left Laine. 'Thank God for that,' she said fervently. And her relief was such that there was nothing she could do about the smile that started from somewhere in the depths of her, and surfaced to part her warm lips, as her mouth picked up at the corners and, not seeing Baldazare Forturini as an adversary but only as the bearer of the best of news, she beamed a smile at him that was little short of beautiful to see.

Indeed, so great was her relief that she was mindless of the intensity of the look from the man who had been aggressive with her from the start; mindless that his eyes were now fixed and held by that first smile he had seen on her. Animosity with him, too, was forgotten—that was until she saw his brow come down, his scowl back just before he moved to half turn from her.

It was then that her smile began to fade. Then, as he turned again to face her, his expression telling her nothing of what was going on behind that clever forehead, she guessed he would be leaving—though not, she felt, without bestowing yet another uncomplimentary remark.

But, aware that she could be hot-tempered on occasions, Laine did not want to be stirred into anger by him again. If anything, she saw that she should be grateful that this busy man had gone out of his way to put her fears about his brother at rest—albeit he had taken his time about it. Quickly then, in an attempt to forestall yet another insult which would see her forgetting her gratitude, she said:

'Thank you so much for telling me what you have,

Signore Forturini.' His arrogant stare told her he could do without her thanks. 'I know how busy you always are,' she rushed on, still trying to avert an insult. 'It was good of you to spare the time . . .'

'My purpose in coming to see you was not, *signorina*, out of the goodness of my heart,' he bluntly cut in to set her straight.

Stopped in her tracks, Laine was still determined to keep her temper. 'Well, I'm grateful just the same,' she told him, and she even managed something of a second smile. Though curiosity was starting to stir, and as her faint smile was noted and she saw the shrewd look that came into those dark eyes, she found she was asking, her chin tilting not a little, 'Was it just to hurl offensive remarks at me that you tore yourself away from whatever business you have in my country?'

For a while she thought he was not going to so much as condescend to reply. But then, just as though he was summing up and had come to some conclusion, she was hearing that she had been a little previous in her cheering that all was well again with Cristo now.

'My brother,' she was told as the tall man went to stand over by the window, 'has been very seriously ill.'

'I know that,' said Laine quietly, her anger fading as she saw how deeply affected he must have been that Cristo had been at death's door. How, man-like, he did not want any stranger to see emotion in his face as he remembered how ill Cristo had been.

'What you do not know,' he said, not so hard and unfeeling as she had thought him she saw as he kept his back to her, 'is that Cristoforo is still extremely weak.'

'Oh,' broke from her. 'I'm so sorry,' she said,

realising that Cristo must have really been through the mill if a month after the crisis had broken he was still in a state of exhaustion.

'Extremely weak,' he repeated, just as though she had not spoken, 'and ...' he paused, and just as though it went against the grain to say it, '... and desperately in need to see you, *signorina*.'

'He wants to see *me*!'

Her exclamation had Baldazare Forturini swinging round. 'Is that so surprising?' he questioned.

From her point of view it was. Surely Oriana would be the person he would more likely want to see. Though Laine had to admit Cristo had lost that lost-love look during the months they had known him.

'Are you sure it's me he needs to see?' she asked, not quite able to accept Cristo being 'desperately in need' to see her. From her point of view, if he wanted to see anyone of the Balfours while he was feeling so low, she would have thought it would be her mother who had treated him as one of her own; who had fussed him and had done more than any of them to help him with his sadness of heart when he had been low before.

'I am not mistaken,' she was curtly told, her doubts that it was her firmly knocked on the head as he went on, 'My brother has described you to me in detail. Do you know any other Elaine who has blonde hair and eyes, navy like a crisp starry night sky?' he questioned, which definitely ruled out her greying, dark-haired, brown-eyed mother, Laine thought, as he went on, 'Do you know another Elaine with a special husky quality of voice which makes a man desperate to hear it again?'

Her brow puckered. Had Cristo really said that? Perhaps in his delirium he had said it, she thought, though she had to concede, 'I'm the only blonde-haired Elaine I know—though my friends always call me Laine. Did Cristo call me Laine?' she queried.

'My brother is not making the progress hoped for,' he announced, her question going unanswered, as with more important things on his mind; against his better judgment, it seemed, he enlightened her, 'It is his physician's opinion that by not seeing you, his recovery is being retarded.'

Still not completely able to see how this could be, Laine knew only then that since this man set so much store by the truth, then the truth must be what he was telling her. And, her heart going out to Cristo again, all she could think was that if it meant so much to him to see her again, then if at all possible, see her he would.

'Is he able to travel?' she asked, eager to do her bit towards his recovery. 'Perhaps a convalescence in England might . . .'

Harshly, when she was getting sick and tired of the way Zare Forturini continually butted in, Laine found herself chopped off again, as once more all aggression, he snarled:

'You are suggesting he moves in with you? Have you not heard a word I have said?'

'You said he was weak,' she replied, trying not to rise at his tone, thinking that to hire a special ambulance flight would not break the wealthy Forturinis.

'Extremely weak, was what I said,' he reminded her sharply, and revealing what he had seen in her remark, but which certainly had not been intended. 'Apart from the temperament of your English climate,' he told her, 'I do not think the exertions entailed in the resumption of being your lover will be efficacious to his return to full strength.'

As she gasped anew, there was no chance then of
Laine holding down her temper. 'Cristo has never
been my lover,' she threw at him angrily. But she was
to see that he was no more ready to believe her than he
had been, as, undaunted by the furious sparks flashing
from her eyes, sneeringly he retorted:

'Nor do you think enough of him to go to Italy to
see him, do you?'

Surprise at his question sent her anger away. She
was uncertain whether he was merely having a go at
her because she had not rushed to Italy at his
telephoned command a month ago, or whether he
could be suggesting that she go to Italy now. Though,
on recalling his 'My purpose in coming to see you was
not out of the goodness of my heart' of only a short
while ago, Laine was seeing that loath though Zare
Forturini might be to ask anything of her, with Cristo
not showing any improvement, asking her to go to his
brother must be exactly what he was doing!

'Er—it—isn't that I wouldn't go to Italy if I could,'
she answered his question at long last, feeling a little
awkward as that same fierce pride which her parents
possessed attacked to prevent her from telling him
outright that she was as broke as made no difference.
'It's just that I—can't, at the moment.'

'Can't or won't?' came hurtling grimly back at her
as, leaving her in no doubt that his 'heartless bitch'
opinion of her had not improved at all, angrily
sarcastic, he asked, 'You have work of vital importance
to the nation which you cannot leave *at the moment*?'

Knowing she was going to go further down the scale
in his estimation—'idle layabout' about to be tacked
on to her charge sheet—Laine's chin tilted as she told
him defiantly:

'I don't happen to have a job at present.'

That did not appear to surprise him. But she was to hear that he had not yet done with his sarcasm, as, 'You have another boyfriend, one who has not found the time to move in yet?' he challenged.

Holding fast on to her temper—that or thump him—Laine clenched her hands at her sides. 'I do have a—friend,' she told him as coolly as she could, Austin again coming in useful when pride demanded that this man shouldn't know that she hadn't had what she would call a proper date since she had decided to rope Austin into her scheming. 'But,' she added, still hanging on to that cool note, 'he's no one I couldn't leave—if I had a mind to.'

'So what's your objection?' he rapped, his glowering expression telling her that he did not think very much of her intimation that she would drop her men friends whenever it suited her. 'Are you waiting for me to offer to pay you to go and see Cristoforo?'

With difficulty, Laine held back on the urge to punch his head. 'Don't be disgusting,' she told him disdainfully. Pride was like a banner before her then, as she went on to let him know that not one halfpenny would she take from him to go on an errand of mercy—but only for her to come a cropper on her high horse when hauteur had her unthinkingly telling him, 'Had I any money, I would be offering to pay *you* to take you and your objectionable self to the remotest part of the . . .'

'You are without funds, *signorina*?' he came in to sharply slice off her word 'universe'.

Inwardly groaning that she had no one to blame but herself, Laine did the best she could to recapture her disdain. 'Temporarily,' she said loftily. And hoping that she had conveyed that her bank had somehow fouled up her account but that as soon as they had sorted out the muddle she would be flush again, she felt better able to try and put him right in his belief that she had no heart. 'Were that not the case, I would not hesitate to go and see Cristo as you suggest.' Purposefully then, she went to the sitting room door and with an airy disdain about her, she pulled it wide. 'Perhaps when next you see your brother, *signore*,' she said, giving him a superior look from beneath her long lashes, 'you will give him my love.'

For perhaps five seconds the autocratic Baldazare Forturini di Montonasco did not move. Then Laine was to find that her disdain was a poor thing by the side of his. Moving swiftly, he was suddenly towering over her as he looked down at her, and he was wasting no more time then on the likes of her, as he let her know that he was nobody's messenger.

'Give your love to him yourself,' he told her icily, cutting through her show of pride as, all decisive, he gritted, 'Perhaps it will not hurt you *too* much to accept a flight ticket from me.'

'You'll pay my air fare?' she questioned, knowing that if she had been bluffing in her haughty statement that she would not hesitate to go to Cristo if she had the wherewithal, then her bluff was being well and truly called.

'Be packed and ready to leave at ten tomorrow morning,' was his concise answer—he did not wait for her to see him out.

Five minutes after she had heard the front door slam shut, Laine was still sitting in the chair she had slumped into. Had she really agreed to go to Italy tomorrow? she had to wonder. Had she indeed—still in her bathrobe—been entertaining that autocratic, aggressive brute at all? Though from what she remembered of it, entertaining was precisely what it had not been.

She wasn't going, of course, she thought another five minutes later. With all that devil thought of her, nothing in the world would have her accepting so much as a bus ticket from him, let alone an airline ticket.

Determined then that whoever the head of the Forturini empire sent to take her to the airport in the morning, she was not going anywhere, Laine had to own to a flicker of something she could not name at her decision.

Surely it wasn't disappointment? A moment later she was having to own that however much she had hated everything that fiend had said to her, it certainly hadn't been dull while he was around. But, remembering how earlier she had been thinking that at twenty-two life should be more exciting than it was, she was then of the opinion that of the two, she by far preferred the little rut she looked like settling in until her parents returned.

Thoughts of the early night she had been going to have were pushed from her mind when, knowing she'd be lucky if she slept at all that night, Laine went and made herself a warm drink.

Cristo came into her thoughts then, and she was glad he had safely made it out of his crisis. But by the sound of it, he still had a long haul in front of him. Though now that his brother was no longer there to breathe fire and fury at her, it seemed odder than ever that she should be the one Cristo so desperately wanted to see!

Aware that she had been pacing up and down only when she found herself by the telephone when it shrilled, Austin, Laine thought, was all she needed. But because she knew full well that if she didn't answer it, Austin would be round full pelt to see if she was all right, with a sigh she picked it up.

Feeling far from 'all right', she heard that it was Austin, his breath in his fist as he told her that he had raced home from the motor-bike scramble with the thought to get cleaned up before he came round to see her.

'Actually, Austin, I'd rather you didn't come round, if you don't mind,' she heard herself find the courage to say.

'You're going to have another early night?' he asked, giving her self-respect in her twenty-two years and her dull existence just recently something of a hefty nudge that by the sound of it, even Austin thought she must be a tired old thing to want to see so much of her bed.

'No, I'm not, actually,' she replied, not a little irritated with the picture of herself he had presented her with. 'But I am rather busy at the moment.'

'Busy!' he repeated, sounding stunned that she was too busy to see him.

'That's right,' said Laine, her heart starting to drum as the excitement that had been lacking in her began to make up for lost time. 'I have some packing to do.'

'*Packing?* Where on earth are you going?'

'As a matter of fact,' she replied, outwardly calm, 'I'm going to Italy—but only for a few days.'

CHAPTER THREE

STARING at the small suitcase reposing on her bed, Laine was still wondering, as she had ever since she had awakened that morning, was she being a complete idiot?

Yet another glance at her watch showed that there were still fifteen minutes to go before she would find out if Zare Forturini had meant it when he had commanded, 'Be ready at ten'.

Would eleven o'clock see her unpacking that small case? Last night she had thought her visit would be of a few days' duration—if that. But in the clear light of day, she was growing more and more of the opinion that she wouldn't be going anywhere at all.

And about that, she did not know whether she was glad or sorry. The excitement that had stirred in her blood last night, that urging in her to live dangerously, to come out from under that safe secure mantle of protection which though for the most part going unnoticed had always been provided by her family, was far from her that morning.

Not that going to Italy to see a sick friend could be termed 'living dangerously', she thought, as she flicked another glance at her watch. Perhaps it was just that crossing swords with Forturini senior had made it seem that way. She had to admit that standing up to him definitely stirred something in the adrenalin. He certainly knew how to draw her anger, at any rate!

Again wondering if he had been serious, glad that no one would know what a fool she had been to pack if he had not been, Laine again went over her conversation with him—though to her mind, it had been more of a one-sided slanging match. She recalled the way he had soon put her right when she had thanked him for coming to tell her how Cristo was. And she had to own, from what she knew of him, that he should come purely to order her to Italy made more sense than that he should call to give her a progress report on his brother.

Which had to mean he was truly concerned about Cristo's health. For with all the terrible things he thought her—money-grubbing and with lovers by the score, to hear him tell it—in normal circumstances he would be more likely to fumigate the air around her before he would let her anywhere near Cristo.

That thought alone told Laine that, no matter how hard he had been on Cristo—and in her view transferring him from Italy and away from Oriana had been terribly cruel—Zare Forturini loved his brother.

Which thought made her unsure again. For, recalling that phone call a month ago when he had made no bones about telling her that his sole purpose in recalling Cristo had been to get him away from her clutches, she was left wondering if that love would prove strong enough that against his better judgment he should supply an airplane ticket for her, with an exact opposite purpose in mind—that purpose of sending her *to* Cristo! A minute later, Laine had her answer.

When, with still three minutes to go before the clock struck ten, the sound of the door bell shrilled through the silent house, she jumped like a scalded cat.

Her thoughts chaotic, not at all sure she would not welcome even dull Austin being on the other side of the door, Laine descended the stairs with a hammering heart as she visualised Austin, some chauffeur or taxi driver there, or even Zare Forturini himself come to personally make sure that she stepped on to that plane.

Though it wouldn't be Zare Forturini, she discounted, as she reached the front door. He was much too busy to see to such a small thing as putting Laine Balfour on a plane. It was obvious that he was in England on business only, but had taken time out to come and see her last night. He certainly wouldn't have any more time to spare for the likes of her, she could be positive on that.

But in that assumption, as she pulled back the door, Laine discovered that she was very wrong. For it was none other than Zare Forturini who stood there, lounge-suited and as sophisticated as ever, as he stared unspeaking and waited to be invited in.

'You were serious, then?' The words had come blurting from her as, her heart racing madly, she knew she would not be unpacking that case upstairs, at least, not until she reached Italy she wouldn't.

'You are ready?' he asked shortly, superbly ignoring her question, a fine look of impatience about him as she stood back and he stepped through the doorway.

'My—c-case is upstairs,' she stammered, nerves getting to her at the last minute as, realising that he had indeed been serious, she began to get cold feet.

'You wish me to collect your case for you?' he questioned, to her mind impossibly arrogant as without waiting for her answer he went striding towards the stairs.

'I can get it,' she said, speeding after him, anger already starting to ignite—and he hadn't been in the house a minute! 'I'm quite capable of carrying my own luggage,' she told him haughtily.

God, what a man! she was thinking, up in her room.

Used to giving his orders, he couldn't wait a minute, could he? Well, he needn't think she was going to jump every time he called 'jump'. Not that she was likely to see him again once he had dumped her at the airport.

But that thought, the thought that once she had said goodbye to him she would then be on her own, made her realise that in her preoccupation with would she or would she not be making the trip, she had given not one thought to what she would do when she got to Italy!

It was quite possible, of course, that arrangements had been made for her to be met at the airport, but what if those arrangements fouled up?—things like that happened sometimes. What if she wasn't being met but was expected to find her way on her own? She had money for neither train nor taxi! Not so much as a single coin in Italian currency did she have with which to make a phone call or try to catch a bus.

As she was taking her case from the bed, another horrifying thought struck. With Zare Forturini hating one Laine Balfour like poison, was it likely he would countenance her putting up for so much as one night under his roof? Naturally she would be going to his home to visit Cristo. But, with that tyrant downstairs thinking she was panting to spend the night sharing Cristo's bed, she'd like to bet anything that he had made arrangements for her to stay in some hotel—and who was supposed to pay for that?

Laine picked up her case and left her room. But whether Zare Forturini was impatient to get rid of her or not, she saw very clearly then that before she so much as set one foot outside the security of her home, whether he thought she was again on the make—and knowing him, that was exactly what he would think—

she was going to have to bring up that dreadful subject—money!

Impatience was stamped on every part of him as, heading down the stairs, she saw he was more or less in the same place she had left him. 'You have a passport?' he thought to ask, his hand coming out automatically to relieve her of her case as she reached him. 'We do not need to stop to get you a twelve-month one?' he questioned, already on his way to the door.

Her non-answer had him turning, to see that she had not moved from the foot of the stairs. 'I have a new ten-year passport,' she replied huskily, pride forming a barrier between her and her need to get the money situation sorted out before she went a step further. 'As yet,' she delayed, 'my passport is unused.'

'You were thinking of going somewhere?' he questioned, as aware as she was that people just didn't apply for passports without any intention of leaving their own country.

'It was not my intention to go to Italy when I applied for it,' she said, trying for sarcasm, but only to discover he would always have an answer ready for her.

'You could have gone far on the two thousand pounds my brother gave you,' came bouncing back.

'Cristo never . . .' she started to storm, the adrenalin pumping. She stopped, seeing the opening her pride had been looking for. 'Talking of money,' she went on, wanting any other conversation but the one she was about to embark upon, 'since I have neither lire nor travellers' cheques, would you mind telling me how I'm supposed to pay my hotel bill?'

'Your hotel bill?' he queried, to annoy her. He knew full well what she was talking about, damn him!

'I haven't even the price of a—a cup of coffee,' she made herself go on, sounding more and more to her ears as though she was asking him for money. 'How— just how am I supposed to get where I'm going when my plane lands?' she asked, sticking grimly in there. And as another thought struck, 'And that's another thing—where *am* I going? That is,' she thought she had better let him know that as yet it was not all so cut and dried as he obviously thought, 'if I'm going at all.'

'You are prepared to let Cristoforo waste away for the sight of you?' he rapped angrily, not liking, she saw, that she looked to be throwing a spanner in the works.

But in having had to accept that Cristo for some reason had a real need to see her, the intimation that Zare Forturini thought she was the last word in callousness had her back-pedalling a little.

'It isn't that I—don't want to see him,' she said, and saw immediately from the dark frown she received that that didn't please him either. 'But—but you must see how—how I'm placed. I don't know if I'm being met or—or if I have to make my own way, and . . .'

Zare Forturini leaving her and going to open the front door had her breaking off and staring after him. But she was positively gasping when, holding the door wide with every expectation of her going through it, he said:

'Do not concern your beautiful head about money, *signorina*,' and while she was wondering if he was being sarcastic, 'Everything to do with your accommodation has been settled. As for who will meet you— there is no need for you to worry about that either. I shall be making the trip with you.'

It must be the sheer force of his personality, Laine thought some while later. For she had no clear recollection of intentionally leaving the stand she had taken at the bottom of the stairs. Yet here she was in the car beside him, with all the signposts she had seen telling her that they were headed in the direction of Gatwick airport.

Or perhaps it was just the shock of knowing that Zare Forturini was to be her travelling companion that, stunned, she had meekly left the house to take the front passenger seat of the limousine parked outside.

Thank goodness the back door of the house was locked, she mused, as the car sped on. Wouldn't the unsmiling, unspeaking man by her side just love it if she'd had to tell him to turn the car around so she could go back and lock up!

A hint of a smile started up inside her at that thought. And it was then that she realised that the anger and frustration in her against the bossy brute must have mellowed. Even annoyance she should have been feeling that she had to put up with him throughout the flight was a non-starter, she found. For how could she continue to be annoyed with him when his concern for Cristo must be so great that he was cutting short his business and journeying to Italy too?

He had probably worked far into the night the sooner to get back to the brother he loved, she found herself thinking. With Cristo not making progress he would not want to be away from home for too long. It must have cut into his work too, to snatch an hour out of his busy Sunday to call at her home, she thought. Not that he had wanted to call, she was under no illusions about that. But Cristo had come first, even if Zare Forturini must be hating it like hell that having sent Cristo away because he had fallen in love with someone he deemed unsuitable, he was having to grin and bear it as he placed him in the clutches of a female who, by telling him that she had not so much as the price of a cup of coffee, must have appeared to be asking him for a handout.

Not liking that thought, Laine had something else to pin her thoughts on in that they had reached the airport. But in thinking that it would take her an hour to sort out which of the many check-in points she should present herself, she was soon seeing that her companion was a seasoned traveller.

Her case weighed in, her boarding card in her hand, her elbow was gripped and she was being directed to yet another area. Here her passport was checked, her person checked electronically for any prohibited article, as was her shoulder-bag, and before she had filed away all these new experiences, that firm hand was at her elbow again and she was being marched into a waiting aircraft.

Trying to make it appear as though she too flew around the world whenever matters arose which just could not be dealt with over the telephone, Laine leaned back in her seat and closed her eyes as the plane took off. Some people said flying was boring, others exciting, her mother frightening. But Laine felt just numb. Because it was then that she realised that it was too late for her to change her mind about wanting to live dangerously. It was only then that she saw that from now until she returned to England, she had committed herself to the dictates of the brutish man sitting next to her!

They had been in the air some time before she came out of her numbed sense of apprehension to remember that in all the many silent moments, when she had meant to ask how Cristo was this morning, she had not done so. It went without saying that Zare Forturini would have put through a call to Italy before he had come to collect her. Which meant that Cristo could not have made any improvement, otherwise she could be certain that she wouldn't be sitting in this aeroplane now.

She turned on a sudden impulse. 'Mr ...' she began, and felt angry with herself, with him, hating him and the arrogant way he turned his unsmiling head. '*Signore* ...' she started off again, but only to be interrupted:

'I should not like my brother to see the hostility you feel for me,' he said coolly, obviously not missing, but uncaring personally of, the daggers he saw in her eyes. 'His way from now on must be without stress. Perhaps,' he suggested, 'you will practise from now until we arrive at our destination, in calling me Zare.'

Like hell she would! Though Baldazare, since she was bound to call him something in Cristo's presence, was rather a mouthful, she thought, thanking him for nothing as it dawned on her that it was more than about time that she knew exactly where she was going to rest her head that night.

'Talking of our destination, *sign* ...' She didn't correct it, the name Zare refusing to leave her lips. 'Would you mind telling me exactly where I'm going?'

His reply, 'Bologna,' had that old familiar urge to set about him starting up again.

'I know *that*,' she told him tartly, not liking at all that he must be baiting her, since she'd have to be dimmer than dim not to have realised by now that Bologna was where the plane was heading. Though on second thoughts, 'Is Bologna where Cristo is?' she asked, a shade puzzled as she tried to conjure up a map of Italy. Surely Bologna was to the north of

Florence. Cristo, she was sure, lived to the south of that beautiful city!

'You cannot wait to get to him?'

The query had come sharply and Laine was angry again. It made him no more endearing to her to know that he thought she couldn't wait to get to Cristo to see what extra pickings there might be to go along with the two thousand pounds she was already supposed to have received.

With difficulty, she controlled her desire to suggest that she wouldn't miss him if he wanted to inspect the outside washroom. 'I merely want to know where I'm going,' she said, expanding in the same taut voice. 'I have an idea that Cristo lives somewhere between Siena and Florence, but . . .'

'You are maintaining still that you have no idea exactly where?' Stubbornly she refused to answer, and realised he was out to needle some response from her as he jibed, 'You let him—escape—without first obtaining his forwarding address?'

God, was he asking for it! Laine fumed. In front of an aircraft almost full to capacity was he pushing his luck! 'Had I known where your brother lived, *signore*,' she told him, her temper straining at the leash—he could take a running jump before she would call him Zare, 'I would have made every effort to enquire as to his wellbeing after you phoned saying how gravely ill he was.'

'You have never heard of directory enquiries?' he asked abruptly.

'I . . .' she halted. 'Is that how you found my number?' she asked.

'It is how I found your address. I rang every English telephone number in my brother's diary until an Elaine answered the number beside the name

Balfour. It was a small matter to get the address that fitted your telephone number.'

Accepting that to search in Cristo's diary was the quickest way to find some clue to the girl who in his delirium he had been raving for, Laine reasserted herself.

'But I didn't so much as have Cristo's telephone number,' she protested. But she could see she could have spared her breath. 'Anyway,' she said, thinking him the most frustrating, aggravating man on earth, 'you still haven't told me where we're going.'

He gave her a look that told her he was not a little fed up with her. Then, perhaps judging from her stubborn look that he would get no peace until he had told her what she wanted to know, he said:

'We are going to my home—where else?'

'And your home is where Cristo is?' she persisted, the bit between her teeth.

'*Si*,' he replied shortly, turning his head from her as if to convey that the conversation was over.

'And that is—where?'

Arrogantly, he turned his proud head. 'Valgaro,' he said curtly.

'Which is somewhere in between Florence and Siena?'

'What a little terrier you are!' he commented.

But suddenly his mouth was showing a faint quirk, as though against his will he found her amusing. Then, to her surprise, whether or not he thought she already knew what he was about to tell her, he was relenting to reveal:

'In actual fact my home is much nearer to Siena than it is to Florence. But,' he paused, pride about him still and—was it love for his home that had that cold look leaving his eyes?—'although the travelling

involved is not always convenient, it is where I like to
live.'

All her antagonism against him suddenly evaporated.
This place Valgaro must be some place, she guessed,
since it appeared he was ready to put up with any
inconvenience to live there. But before she could ask
how far it was from Siena, he was telling her, 'We are
descending,' and as though he thought her hands were
paralysed, without more ado he was bending to fasten
up her seatbelt.

That Bologna airport was only tiny in comparison
with Gatwick was about all Laine had time to note.
For no sooner had their plane come to a stop than her
tall sophisticated companion had whisked her through
the control points and outside to where a limousine
similar to the one he had driven in England awaited
them.

But then, strangely, where other Italian traffic
seemed to be tearing around, Zare Forturini appeared
in no particular hurry to reach their final destination.

This was borne in on her when, after a couple of
hours of passing through town and countryside,
without bothering to ask if she was hungry, which she
was not, he pulled the car into the forecourt of a
smart-looking hotel, only then thinking to tell her:

'We will dine here.'

'I ate on the plane,' she reminded him, just in case it
put him out of countenance that she didn't have much
of an appetite.

'You enjoy airline meals?' he enquired, already
ushering her inside the building.

From that she guessed he thought she was a
connoisseur of meals served on the various airlines. She
didn't think he would believe her if she told him that that
afternoon's meal was the first sample she'd had.

It was typical of his high-handed methods, she thought, that he ordered for her. Not that she would have understood the Italian menu, but it wouldn't have hurt him to consult her.

'Eat well,' he instructed, when she had finished a delicious soup and had her main course before her. 'I told Anna-Maria not to bother with a meal for us tonight. Though of course,' he added in the manner of the perfect host, that faint quirk of a smile almost making it again, 'she will be able to find you something to fill a hollow corner if you are hungry when we arrive.'

Thinking that if she ate all that was before her she would still be full this time tomorrow, his mention of Anna-Maria brought back the memory of the many conversations she had had with Cristo.

'Anna-Maria,' she said, taking a sip of the wine her escort had poured for her, and not certain if she liked it, 'she's hour housekeeper, isn't she?'

'My brother has told you of her?' he enquired, his expression for the first time, she saw, not darkening when Cristo came into the conversation.

Laine nodded, taking another sip of her wine and thinking how much the flavour was improving the more her palate got used to it. 'From what I can remember, I think Cristo has a soft spot for Anna-Maria.'

'The same can be said of my housekeeper,' he unbent sufficiently to tell her, his manners a vast improvement, she noted, now that they were surrounded by people who could witness his impatience with her. 'I don't think it would be an overstatement,' he went on, 'to say that from the time he was a baby, Anna-Maria has doted on that young man.'

With Zare Forturini putting aside his dislike of her

while they were in company, Laine ploughed through what she could of her meal. She observed that they looked just like any other couple and not the antagonists that they were as she learned that both Anna-Maria and her sister Angelina worked for the Forturinis at Valgaro. Anna-Maria, she discovered as her host stayed on his best behaviour, was a widow. Though Angelina's husband was alive and well, and also was employed at the house.

Darkness had fallen when they came from the hotel. And, when they were on their way again, Laine guessed that though she was still clear-headed, the wine must be responsible for the fact that she was feeling a little sleepy.

The purr of the car was having a soporific effect too, she thought, as a few miles farther on she found it was an effort to keep her eyes open.

Her last waking thought was that she still hadn't asked how Cristo was, but that she had no need to ask. Though oddly, since he must still be very low or she would not be on her way to him, Zare Forturini wasn't exactly putting his foot to the floorboards the sooner to see for himself how his brother fared, was he?

A hand, a warm gentle hand stroking down the side of her smooth unblemished cheek, brought Laine awake, and she realised that the car had stopped. Her next realisation as she opened her eyes was that the feel of a warm gentle hand caressing her face must have been part of some safe secure dream of which she had no recollection. For there was nothing warm or caressing in the cool voice that came to her as Zare Forturini moved her from where she had fallen against his shoulder, and announced:

'We have arrived, *signorina*.'

Shaken to discover that she had been using him for

a pillow. Laine came rapidly awake. 'I'm sorry,' she began to mumble, but by then he was out of the car, her apology going unheard as he collected their cases, his a small one like hers, she had noted, then ushered her to where a porch light was beaming out a welcome.

Laine's head then became a confusion of impressions as they went into a wide hall and, her eyes adjusting to the light, she saw two plump ladies very similar in appearance come forward. Then as Zare addressed the two women in a fast flow of Italian, she saw that a man some fifty to sixty years old was following in their wake.

Picking out Cristo's name in what Zare was saying, she saw that in his sudden urgency to know how his brother was, he had cut short any greeting the trio would have made.

Not knowing any Italian, she was left to glean what she could of the latest report on Cristo's health from their faces as, like lightning, Italian flew back and forth. Then as Zare's enquiries were answered, apparently, Laine had been able to glean very little save that one of the women had a gentle expression on her face when she replied something about 'Signor Cristoforo'.

Her assumption that this one must be Anna-Maria proved correct when, his good manners surfacing, her host introduced his staff. As she shook hands with each one in turn, the question Laine wanted to ask of 'How is Cristo?' was delayed. And by the time English and Italian 'How do you do's' had been exchanged, she was still no nearer finding out how he was.

For with Anna-Maria, Angelina and Giuseppe still standing there, Zare Forturini changed swiftly to English and was telling her, his expression showing none of how the news of Cristo had affected him:

'Come with me—I will take you to your room.'

Laine hared up the stairs behind his long-legged strides, purely because she had too. Annoyance flicked her that, when he must see what she had been about to ask, Zare Forturini was back to being high-handed again.

Not that she could take any exception to the room he was already standing in when she panted in after him, for it was palatial and beautiful. No expense had been spared on thick carpeting or in the rich furnishings. Feminine touches had been added here and there, evidenced in the bed that had been turned down to expose the fine handmade lace that edged the bedlinen.

But, while she owned that the turned-back bed did look inviting, it was not, Laine fumed, for her own comfort that she had been brought there.

'*Signore* . . .' was as far as she got before, back to chopping her off again, he cut in:

'Anna-Maria will arrive shortly with some refreshment for you. Then, *signorina*, you may climb into your bed and finish off the sleep you began in . . .'

'I do not wish to climb into my bed.' How satisfying it was to chop him off for a change! But he was in there again before she could take more than a moment's pleasure from her feeling of satisfaction.

'You do not like your room?' he questioned, wrongfooting her so that she was on the defensive, when on the defensive was not where she wanted to be.

'It's not that,' she found herself saying. 'The room is delightful,' she added, knowing that having seen her rather threadbare home, he must know that. But pride that anyone might look down on her home, even if there had been nothing about him to suggest anything of the sort, had her anger flaring. Abruptly she came off the defensive to declare aggressively, 'I want to see Cristo.'

The darkening of his expression, even if it was solely that Cristo should see her with all haste that she had been brought there, told Laine that not only was he still hating the necessity of putting his brother in her orbit again, but that her manner of speaking to him had made *him* angry with *her*.

Though if she had made him angry, then what Zare Forturini replied sent the heat in Laine rocketing to be boiling hot fury.

'Perhaps it is that you are missing something from your lover,' he snarled, taking an aggressive pace forward, his chin jutting as he added without apology, 'You must be desperate, *signorina*, that before you have been in my home five minutes, you cannot wait to know his room so that you may climb in between the sheets with him!'

Staggered, Laine could not believe what she was hearing. But he was making her believe she had heard what she thought she had, and succeeded in sending her fury soaring when, only a pace away, still no nearer to looking apologetic, he reminded her savagely:

'Have you forgotten—I have already told you—my brother is not yet strong enough for such—antics.'

Crack! Her hand starting to sting told Laine she had just served Baldazare Forturini di Montonasco what he had been asking for ever since she had first heard the sound of his voice. But, his fury on the loose at being served such a vicious swipe, as fierce hands shot out to take her arms in an unbreakable grip, Laine knew she was not going to be allowed to get away with it.

'So I was right!' hissed through his clenched teeth.

'There *is* an excess of passion in you!' And with a fire burning in his dark eyes she found frightening, he jerked her close up to him as he gritted, 'Permit me, *signorina*, to help you work off some of that passion!'

And before she could attempt to stop him, the light was abruptly blotted out, and in the next moment fierce angry lips had claimed hers.

With his arms like iron bands around her, Laine's struggles to be free proved useless. Kiss after punishing kiss he pressed on her mouth, refusing to let her move a fraction out of his crushing hold.

How long it went on, Laine had no idea. But suddenly, whether he became aware of her breasts crushed up against his chest and in doing so that he might be causing her pain, while keeping her firmly to him, he released sufficient pressure to let her breathe. Then it was that the tenor of his kisses began to change.

And all at once Laine was forgetting to be angry. This new, gentler way of his kissing her was having the strangest effect on her. His hold, almost tender now, was making her body react in the most peculiar fashion, so that she was no longer straining to get away from him but straining to get even closer to him!

When suddenly Zare ceased that sensual movement of his mouth over hers, then abruptly put her from him, Laine was little short of incredulous to discover that she had actually been *responding* to him!

He knew it too! He did not have to say anything. Just that look in his experienced eyes as he stood back and without a word, quietly looked at her, was all she needed to know that he knew all about the emotions he had triggered off in her.

And that made her absolutely livid. Furious with herself, furious with him, all the hate she was capable of was in her then at what Zare had been able to do to her. Her colour scarlet, her only defence lay in letting that anger spill over.

'Two of us can play at that game!' She went into battle, hoping for her pride's sake that he would think her response had been nothing more than play-acting. 'So now we've got that charade out of the way—both of us being punished for our actions—you can either do as I asked and take me, this minute, to see Cristo—or,' she said, starting to feel better, 'you can jolly well take me straight back to the airport!'

To have the arrogant devil rock loftily back on his heels when she had thought she had just gained the uipper hand was not, to her way of thinking, the way it was supposed to go at all. But, had she not feared another attempt to exorcise her excess of passion if she took another swing at him, Laine knew, as she felt a fresh impulse to thump him, that that was exactly what she would have done. Though that feeling was to depart and leave shock only in its place, when coolly, not a dent in him, he drawled:

'You, Signorina Balfour, have just got to be joking if you think I am going to drive all the way back to the airport again.' And while it was fast sinking in that when it came to upper hands, then it wasn't she who was holding it, 'You are here in my home,' he added, 'and here, little lady, without lire to pay for even a cup of coffee, is where you will stay—until I say differently!'

Made speechless by what he had just said, her eyes going wide as recognition hit that instinct had been right to make her feel threatened that first time she had seen him, Laine still had not found her voice when, with an insincere smile, Zare Forturini quietly walked out.

CHAPTER FOUR

LAINE opened her eyes on Tuesday to a morning that promised to be sunny. But the mood she had awakened in was far from sunny.

Late and long had she mutinied against the impossible Zare Forturini before sleep had claimed her. But, as she got out of bed intending to take the quickest of showers, she was not at all surprised to find that she still had not done with laying her tongue to names for that particular man.

Faint sounds from below told her that she was in a house of early risers. Well, she was an early riser too, and since she wasn't going to stay a moment longer than she had to, to her mind the sooner she started making plans for her return flight, the better.

Not that she was going to waste her time approaching Zare Forturini for her return ticket to England. But wasteful though it might be when, hating her and all he thought she stood for, she could be certain he had not booked her ticket for one way only, she was going to ask that arrogant swine for nothing. She wouldn't forget in a hurry that look in his eyes after he had put her away from him last night. That all-knowing look that said as clearly as if he had spoken it, 'So—you turn on for anybody!'

Wishing she had hit him harder, Laine took a quick shower, wishing at the same time that she could as quickly put the way he'd made her want to get yet closer to him as nothing more than a need in her to lean against something through being dead tired from her journeyings that day.

But, with an honesty in her which she could well do without, she owned that when the tenor of his kisses had changed—and heaven alone knew what had got into her—far from feeling travel-weary, she had never felt more alive in her life.

Memory of that warm sensual mouth over hers made her concentrate hard on Cristo, as, leaving her bathroom, she donned trousers and a light sweater.

For two pins she would have gone searching for Cristo after that lofty devil, with his insincere smile, had sauntered from her room. Only the thought that Cristo might have been given a sleeping draught the better for him to have a restful night had stopped her.

But, she determined, flicking a final comb through her shining blonde hair, then leaving her room, she was going to see him this morning. Mutiny accompanied her as she walked the long landing, then headed down the wide stairs, and she knew she was going to have to go against what, though it was instinctive in her anyway, she had been taught at her mother's knee—that the quickest way to lose friends was to borrow money from them. For, subject to how she found Cristo, soon she would be asking him to loan her the air fare home.

There was, she considered, as she reached the bottom of the stairs, great satisfaction coming her way. For what greater satisfaction could there be when, with her air fare in her pocket, she thumbed her nose at the high and mighty Zare Forturini?

Angelina suddenly appearing saved Laine from going to look for her. But before she could try and get through to her that she would like to be taken to see Signor Cristoforo, Angelina was smilingly indicating that she should follow her.

Guessing that it would not be to Cristo's room that Angelina would be taking her, Laine was all at once remembering the way Zare Forturini, disliking her as he did, had hidden his animosity, and had done nothing to make her look small in the hotel they had dined in, or in front of his servants.

Sighing at her weakness in giving him the benefit of her own good manners, Laine followed the plump Angelina to where she was opening one of the many doors in the hall.

It was here that Laine saw the man she had been hopeful of not having to come into contact with again before she left. But good manners having got her this far, and with Angelina hovering just behind her, Laine did her best to get over the memory of his mouth over hers when he rose from the breakfast table and she saw that it was to her mouth that his glance was flicked, before, leaving her unsure whether he was being sarcastic or not, he said:

'Good morning, *signorina*. You slept well, I trust?'

'Dreamlessly,' she answered with all the cool she could muster. And belatedly, 'Good morning,' grateful, as he indicated that she should take a place at the breakfast table, that Angelina broke into a spate of Italian.

Since it did not look as though he was going to return to his chair until she was seated, there was nothing for it, Laine saw, if Angelina was to remain in ignorance of the hostility she felt for her master, but to take her place by the table setting.

Zare Forturini resumed his seat as soon as she had sat down, and it was then that she heard what the spate of Italian had been about.

'Angelina is anxious to know what you would like for your breakfast,' he said, when Laine had far more important things on her mind.

But since she couldn't get out of it, she managed to murmur, 'I—usually have toast and coffee at home,' and saw that her figure was given the once-over as if to say he thought she wouldn't get very fat on just that.

Suppressing a fresh spurt of mutiny, Laine found her good manners holding up in that they allowed her to send a smile to Angelina as, her wishes translated into Italian, the maid bustled out.

'Perhaps you will not mind sharing my coffee until your breakfast arrives,' said her host, startling her that not only was he sounding equable, but that if her eyes were not playing her false, he was coming down from his lofty perch to personally pour her a cup.

The edge taken off her antagonism by his action, she mumbled a polite, 'Thank you,' then saw that since he apparently was not going to be the one to start hostilities this morning, she might fare better, since she might as well ask him where Cristo's room was, if that question was brought out without the aggression that he had always been sharp to meet.

'Might I know, *signore* . . .' she began, her polite-sounding words halting, as with her hand on the cup and saucer he was passing over, his eyes met hers.

'*Signore?*' he queried, that hint of a quirk about his mouth there again, a sudden charm she had never before seen there too, as he reminded her that he had invited her to call him 'Zare'.

'Er—Zare,' she managed, not understanding the unexpected leap in her heart that by the look of it one night spent back in his home was all that was required to have the sourness in him departing. 'What I wanted to ask,' she went on, 'is—when may I see Cristo?'

For the most part Cristo's name had only ever been effective in bringing out the very worst in the man opposite her, Laine recalled, as with her question out in the open, she waited for his charm to disappear. But she was fast learning that Zare Forturini was a man of constant surprises, for there was a charm about him still as, unbending to call his brother by the same shortened version of his name that she used, his look regretful, he replied:

'I am afraid it will not be possible for you to see Cristo for a little while.'

Fleetingly Laine thought that perhaps a nurse was attending to him at this very moment—though she had seen no evidence of a nurse. But some unspoken nuance in Zare Forturini's reply, had her wondering if 'for a little while' meant she could not see him for half an hour or so, or if it was meant to convey that she could not see his brother for the whole of that morning!

Wanting to be on her way back to England with all speed, only just did she remember her thought that her dealings with this man might be more civilised if she hung back on the hostility he aroused in her.

'Why, *Sign* . . . Zare?' she asked politely. 'Why must I wait to see him?' she pressed, her instinct wary the longer it took for him to answer. 'It is, after all,' she pointed out when still no answer came her way, 'the reason why I'm here—to see Cristo.' And, bridling in spite of herself as she recalled those foul remarks he had barked at her in her room last night, she added tartly, 'I assure you I won't disturb him—in any way—if he's resting. Just tell me which room is his.'

Her astonishment was to be two-fold when, expecting him to jump down her throat, not only did he not retaliate, but it seemed he had been deliberating whether to tell her or not, when he remained calm to advise quietly:

'It would do you no good whatsoever to know where his room is. You see, Cristo is—not here.'

'*Not here?*' Stunned, it was a second or two before Laine had sufficient wind to add anything to her exclamation. Then, 'What am I doing here if Cristo isn't ...' She broke off, instinct running riot, her senses a mixture of fear and anger, until, his voice quiet still, Zare Forturini was there to put some light in her confusion.

'My brother was here,' he explained, 'but yesterday afternoon, to my sorrow, he suffered a relapse.'

'A relapse?' she echoed, her anger disappearing in an instant, as fear for Cristo's life gripped her.

'I'm afraid so,' said Zare, his eyes now fixed on the coffee-pot—his way, she saw, of keeping the emotion he must feel hidden. 'Fortunately,' he went on after a moment, 'Anna-Maria has watched him like a hawk in my absence. She had a doctor here at the first sign that all was not well. The doctor straight away had him re-admitted to hospital.'

'He's in hospital!'

'They have all the up-to-date machinery there,' he explained patiently, letting her know that had it not been for that life-saving machinery, no way would he have let his brother be nursed back to health anywhere but at home.

But as he let her see that, Laine was able to see something else as well. Then she was able to see that, having been somewhere over Europe when Cristo's condition had worsened, Zare had not known any of it until they had arrived last night. To be greeted by such terrible news in answer to his first question of how was Cristo, was the reason for the way he had been with her. For, male-like, unable to break down as perhaps a woman might on hearing such news about a loved one, he had found release in aggression towards the female who he thought was taking his brother for a ride.

'I'm so sorry,' was all she could say for a second or two. Then tears were pricking the backs of her eyes as she said gently, 'But I do wish you could have told me last night.'

That extra husky quality in her voice had him raising his eyes before she could hide the shine of tears in hers. And she guessed, when she saw him frown, that he was wondering why a girl like her should ever look moist-eyed when it was not to her advantage.

'I . . .' he began, then pushed his plate from him, as looking away from her, he confessed, 'I was shaken—he is my only brother.'

Laine had been fighting hard to stop the tears from falling even before she had witnessed that Zare Forturini had no belief that she was sensitive to not only Cristo's suffering, but to his too. But as his voice faded, seeing his suffering in that statement that Cristo was his only brother, she was putting behind her that he had no opinion of her, and was having to swallow hard before she could ask:

'You've seen Cristo—been in touch with the hospital?' Her question, she saw, had been an unnecessary one. He must have thought so too, she saw when he did not answer. 'How is he this morning?' she asked, refraining from asking another unnecessary question of had he telephoned since he had got up—quite likely, being worried—he hadn't been to bed.

'There is no change,' he said quietly.

So poor Cristo still had a battle on his hands. 'May I see him?' she asked, the question a natural one, she thought, when, not only wanting to help if she could, she knew the circumstances of her being there were only so that the sight of her should aid Cristo's recovery.

But her question had Zare Forturini tossing his napkin down on to the table and getting to his feet. And he was already on his way to the door when, bluntly, he told her:

'He is too ill to see anyone but family.'

A flicker of annoyance at being snubbed inserted itself in between Laine and her wanting to help if she could. 'You're going to the hospital now?' she delayed him when, without another word, he would have gone through the door. 'You're going to see Cristo?' she asked, an edge to her voice as pride warred with the dislike of having been put very firmly in her place.

By the time she heard a car start up, Laine's sensitivities had been pulled in several directions. It was all very well to appreciate that to put his mind to work could be one way of Zare's taking his thoughts off his brother being so ill again. But did he have to bark at her just as though she had accused him of being a playboy, 'I have business to attend to,' before he strode off?

As she ate the breakfast Angelina had brought her, Laine's thoughts were divided between Cristo and the other Forturini who had soon lost his charm when aggressively he had let her know that not everybody was the loafer she had given him the impression she was.

Regretting that she had for a minute been taken in by his charm, or that she had made excuses for his aggression with her last night, Laine found she needed some sort of action which would stop her mind from staying with just how incredible *she* had been last night.

To be shooed from the kitchen, both Anna-Maria and Angelina looking horrified at any suggestion that she help out with a few chores, sent her spirits lower than they had been when she had first awakened. Having no wish to return to her room, pleasant though it was, Laine decided to take a look around outside.

As she left through a rear door, it was the sight of Giuseppe starting up a Land Rover that first met her eyes. And it was on him that she practised her *'Buon Giorno.'*

An involuntary smile came to her as his toothy smile came out and he returned her good morning, with a *'Buon giorno'* of his own, tacking on the word *'signorina,'* before he set the vehicle in motion and went off on some errand.

But her fed-up feeling of having nothing to do and all day to do it in was soon fading. For as she walked away from the garage area, and as she was something of a dendrologist, her attention was caught and held by a splendid wood of tall stately trees.

Time ceased to exist then as she stood admiring cypresses, poplar and willow, but eventually she turned her glance to the wide expanse of lawn to the right of her, and her vision then was taken up with a delight of other images.

And in no time she was forgetting every word laid down in childhood by her father of, 'Don't walk across the lawn, walk around it,' and was going to inspect a blaze of colour where cabbage white butterflies danced unhurried, where bees were busy going from flower to glorious coloured flower.

Drawn to investigate further, feeling a compulsion to be part of the tranquil scene, Laine moved across the grass, her feet without conscious instruction from her brain, and she had still not looked her fill when she raised her eyes to the view.

Her breath catching, she saw that while the house had been built on a hill, way in the distance were other hills, lush green carpets interspersed with more beautiful trees stretching out before her. And to her mind then there was only one way to describe the magical setting where Zare Forturini had his home, and that was—enchanting.

No wonder he did not mind the travelling or the inconvenience involved, she thought. In a fairytale spot such as this, she wouldn't mind what inconvenience she was put to so long as she knew that she could come home to this idyllic setting.

The sun had clouded over when Laine found, there seeming no end to the verdant turf beneath her feet, that she had wandered to the front of the house. It was there that, as she thought she would never tire of the view, even were she to live there permanently, she saw the Land Rover making its way back up the hill. A glance at her watch told her that Giuseppe had been away for a couple of hours and that she had never noticed the time passing!

Her mind still full of all she had seen, she went back indoors only when a light rain began to fall, though a shrub of forsythia had her pausing on her way, to her mind its brilliant yellow doing excellent stand-in duty for the sun.

But in her room thoughts that had been kept at bay by the wonderland she had discovered started to encroach. Though some of her worry about Cristo was to ebb when Anna-Maria came to tell her cheerfully, '*Mangiare, signorina, per favore,*' signing with knife and fork actions that lunch was ready. For surely, thought Laine, as she went with her to the dining room, Anna-Maria would not be looking so cheerful if Cristo had not made some improvement?

Disposing of a first course of a deliciously cooked spaghetti, sure that Zare would be fitting in a visit to the hospital before he returned home, Laine found herself wondering what he was doing about his lunch.

Not that she was bothered whether he ate or starved, she thought, as a smiling Anna-Maria came in to take her used dishes and place a second course in front of her.

Convinced as she was that, doting on Cristo as she did, every few hours would have the housekeeper ringing the hospital, it was the cheerful expression on Anna-Maria's face that prompted Laine to set herself the uphill task of finding out how he was.

But her question of, 'Signor Cristoforo, is he *improvo*?' was met with a puzzled stare as Anna-Maria did her best to sort out what the English *signorina* was trying to say.

'Signor Cristoforo—er—*molto*—er . . .' Anna-Maria broke off to do some improvised coughing, which left Laine little the wiser as to whether Cristo was still coughing, or if he had now finished coughing.

'*Grazie*, Anna-Maria,' she thanked her, to terminate a conversation that had never got started.

Though later that afternoon, as she observed from the *sala* window that Angelina was talking to Giuseppe at work in the garden, the sound of someone softly singing made Laine think, since it could only be Anna-Maria who was singing so contentedly, that what the housekeeper had meant to convey was that Cristo had now lost his chest infection.

Her mind easier about him, Laine was back in her room when the sound of a car told her that Zare Forturini had returned. Acting on the impulse to go straight away to find out if she was right to feel easier about Cristo, she was at her door when she halted. Too clearly did she remember then the short shrift she had been served with before when questioning him about his brother. Understandably he was worried, but if she was wrong and Cristo was still fighting for his life, she guessed that she would get short shrift again.

Anyway, she thought, coming away from the door, she would most likely be seeing him at dinner, so she could put her enquiry then when he would be less likely to snarl at her than if she collared him the minute he came in.

When, bathed and changed into a light wool dress, eight o'clock came and went, Laine still sat in her room, starting to form the opinion that maybe no one ate anything after midday in the Forturini household.

A firm knock at her door when her watch said it would soon be eight-thirty told her that dinner was served later in this household than in her own. Not wanting to keep Anna-Maria waiting, Laine scooted over to open the door—but only to find that it was not Anna-Maria who stood there.

'You will join me for dinner,' Zare Forturini stated rather than asked, standing tall and straight and all male in his lightweight suit as he surveyed her, the blue of her dress giving an added brightness to the colour of her eyes.

'Thank you,' she replied, trying to read what news there was from the hospital in his face.

But his expression was telling her little, save that since he was waiting to escort her downstairs, he was doing his best to be polite to a personally unwanted, however necessary, guest in his home.

Fairly tall herself, Laine felt dwarfed as she came out on to the landing and walked beside him, shaking her head in reply, when at the *sala* door he paused to ask her if she would like a drink of something before dinner.

Taking her at her word, he then took her to where she had eaten her lunch, attentively pulling out her chair and waiting for her to be seated before he went round to his own chair.

And Laine was waiting no longer than it took Anna-Maria to serve them with soup from a tureen and to leave them, before she was asking:

'How is Cristo?'

Zare finished breaking off the piece of bread in his hands, before he replied, then, 'There is no change in his condition,' he told her levelly. And to let her know that he had no wish for a discussion about Cristo to be a mealtime conversation piece, he took up the carafe in front of him and asked, 'Wine?'

Impatiently she shook her head, her thoughts troubled that she must have misread the signs in Anna-Maria that Cristo was improving.

'But Anna-Maria was singing,' she blurted out in protest at her disappointment. And when he looked at her as though to say what had that got to do with the price of coal, she was forced to explain, 'She wouldn't have been singing unless your brother was getting better.'

'Anna-Maria is always singing,' came his reply as, taking no heed that she had said she didn't want a drink, absently Zare Forturini filled her wine glass.

He's worried, truly worried about Cristo, Laine thought, as she watched his action in filling her glass. And she was sure that his brother's condition was too painful for him to dwell on, when, as Anna-Maria came in with the serving dishes for the next course, adroitly he switched the conversation.

'Tell me, Laine,' she hid her surprise that he was calling her by the name she had told him her friends used, 'do you have any brothers?'

'One,' she replied, deciding that since it pained him so much to dwell on Cristo it wouldn't hurt her to go along with him. 'Tony lives in Australia,' she followed on as he took up the serving implements and helped her to steak and vegetables. 'That's enough, thank you,' she said, stopping him when he had placed on her plate all she thought she could manage.

Waiting until he had served himself before she started on her own meal, she answered his conversational question of did her brother like living in Australia, then picked up her knife and fork, as, still conversational, Zane asked if she had any sisters.

'My sister Nanette lives in New Zealand,' she answered, quietly thinking that this was one way to get through a meal, and quite probably better than a stony silence, and even finding she was relaxed enough to give him a grin when he remarked:

'Might I guess that your parents live in New Guinea?'

'Wrong,' she replied, her white even teeth in evidence as her lips parted. She saw his eyes were arrested by her mouth, and realised then that if he was very sparing with his smiles, she had not been exactly flush with hers either. 'Though,' she went on to concede, 'my parents are not in England at the moment.'

She was cutting into her steak, observing that he was doing the same with his, when he tossed the conversational ball back:

'Your parents are overseas on holiday?'

Laine nodded while she emptied her mouth of a piece of meat. 'Sort of,' she said when she could. 'They're visiting both Nanette and Tony for a while.'

She was about to cut into her steak again, but her movements ceased when, his voice changing from

conversational to become sharp, abruptly Zare
Forturini rapped:

'You live with your parents in normal times?'

Not liking his sudden change of tone, or that hint of
aggression lurking in the background, Laine felt her
relaxed manner leave her.

'Sorry to disappoint you,' she snapped. 'I know you
would by far prefer to think of me as the type who
doesn't hesitate to shack up with any man I care to—
but yes, in normal times, I live in that house you
visited with my parents.'

Had she expected an apology for what she knew he
had thought? Then as she saw the alert look that had
come to him, Laine knew, as she suspected he was
dissecting what else he knew about her, that she could
whistle before he would say he was sorry.

But in having thought that polite table conversation
was at an end, she was to discover that, while certain
that his brain cogs never had a moment in which to
collect rust, that whatever thoughts had gone through
his head, his voice had gone back to being politely
urbane, as he said:

'Your passport is a new one, you said,' no
aggression there at all. 'Were you perhaps thinking of
travelling to Australia and New Zealand with your
parents?'

Realising his aggression had gone into hiding, Laine
was finding that her own aggression was not standing
up. And suddenly, not liking the feeling that she had
to be forever on her guard with him, she was seeing
that here might be an opportunity to let this man see
that there was nothing in her of the female he had
thought her from the beginning.

So it was that she told him honestly, 'I was going to
go with them, actually. Well, to New Zealand

anyway,' she amended. Starting to feel relief at his encouraging look, she saw that soon he would be seeing her as she really was, and she was confiding, 'I'd even arranged to have three months' leave from my job, but . . .' she broke off, hesitating as the words to tell him she had given her money to her parents refused to be uttered.

The expression that crossed Zare Forturini's face, when still the words stuck in her throat, told her that he thought she was hesitating only because she was making it up as she went along. And Laine could only be glad then that she had not told him that very private reason why she had had to stay at home. She was even appalled that she had come so close to telling him, for as his face darkened and he glowered at her, she could see he would never have believed her had she tried.

'I thought you told me you did not have a job,' he accused harshly, obviously considering he had given her more than enough time to invent another lie, she thought.

Woodenly, knowing he would never believe she would part with a penny of any money she could get her sticky paws on, Laine felt familiar mutiny rising up in her.

'I don't have a job,' she said waspishly. 'Not for the next two months, anyway.' And, her voice still tart, she reminded him, 'I've only just finished telling you—I'm on three months' leave from my work.'

'And what did you tell your employers?' he wanted to know, suspiciously, so that she was back to wanting to thump him. 'That you wished to travel with your parents?'

'What else would I tell them?' she snapped, wondering why she didn't start lying her head off, since clearly he wasn't believing the truth.

'Your parents,' he went on to question disagreeably, 'presumably, were expecting you to go with them—what reason did you give them for backing out?'

'I told them——' she started to snap, but hesitated again. She flushed as she realised that, having been honest this far, if she carried on in this truthful vein, if she told him what she had told her parents, all she would succeed in doing would be to prove to him what a little liar she could be—even if she was still of the opinion that the end had very definitely justified the means. 'As a matter of fact,' she said, aware he had noticed her flare of pink colour and needed no better confirmation that she didn't care whom she strung along, 'I told them that I wouldn't mind not leaving England just then.'

Sternly he stared at her and, blade-sharp, did not begin to cover him. For as his aggression started to peak, she was to learn that not one word of what she had told him had he forgotten, and that the only thing he looked like believing was that last lie she had told her parents.

'You cancelled your arrangements because you thought it more profitable to stay behind with this new man you took up with before my brother's jet plane had left its vapour trail,' he fired.

At that, her aggression rose to meet his head-on. 'I didn't tell them about the profit I was hoping to gain,' she flared sparks flying from her eyes as, furious, she confirmed, 'But they went away thinking my heart was involved with my new boy-friend.'

'Heart!' he exploded derisively, fury in him as he charged, 'You don't care a damn who you lie to, do you?'

'Not if it gets me what I want,' she retorted, the pink colour in her cheeks now that of anger.

'That includes lying to the new boy-friend, doesn't it?' he thundered before she could draw another breath. 'What tale did you tell him? No doubt you were in touch with him in between my visit to your home on Sunday and my coming to collect you yesterday morning.'

'Naturally.'

Too angry to stay seated, she saw a matching fury in him as he too threw his chair to one side, and they stood glaring at each other. She was careless then that he had grown angrier because she had admitted being in touch with her boy-friend in the short time between Sunday night and ten the next morning—all on account of the two-timing he thought she was carrying on behind Cristo's back. For she had just about had enough of Zare Forturini, and before she sailed out of the room in a blaze of temper, she was hurling at him.

'For your information, Baldazare Forturini di Montonasco, I told him that I'd met the most perfect Italian gentleman.' Her hand was already on the door knob when over her shoulder she hissed, 'Believe me, that's the biggest lie I've *ever* told!'

CHAPTER FIVE

BY the Friday of that same week Laine, to put it mildly, was not a little sick of hanging around waiting to see Cristo. She still found the place where she was living enchanting, but what with neither Anna-Maria nor Angelina allowing her to do a hand's turn, and with all her offers to help Giuseppe in the garden being turned down, time was beginning to weigh very heavily.

She was over her fury with Zare Forturini last Tuesday, though not another scrap of information about herself had she given him. Not that there was much more to tell, but with him doubting there was a grain of truth in anything she told him, she was in no mind to feed him ammunition which he could fire back at her in that delightfully accusing manner he had.

On Wednesday Cristo had still been too ill to see anyone but family. And Laine had accepted that. But last night when Zare had come home, not waiting until she saw him at dinner, she had hurried down the stairs to ask once again how Cristo was.

Briefcase in hand, Zare had looked down at her from his lofty height, and she had expected some stinging insult to come winging her way that she had hardly waited for him to get indoors before she wanted to know how her ex-lover, ex-financial backer was faring. Mutiny had entered her soul then, a determination coming that she was not going to accept meekly today that Cristo was too poorly to see only family. Zare had seen the mutiny in her, of course, but it hadn't made his answer any more acceptable.

'He is much the same,' he had replied, not a glimmer of a smile about him, as, astounding her that that was all he was going to tell her, he went to stride away along the wide hall.

Only she wasn't having that. She had come to Italy with the sole purpose of seeing Cristo, certain at the time that within a very few days she would be back in England. Yet here she was having already spent four days waiting to see Cristo—his need to see her desperately urgent, so she had been told—and she just wasn't of a mind to wait any longer.

'Just a moment, *signore*,' she called to his departing back, not liking at all the arrogant way he looked at her as, turning in his stride, he paused momentarily. 'I'd like to talk to you if you can spare me a minute of your time,' she said, her determination to do just that showing as she ignored his superior attitude.

'I'm afraid, *signorina*,' he replied after a moment, his calling her *signorina* telling her that he wasn't feeling very friendly towards her either, 'that any conversation between us will have to wait.'

That well known feeling of wanting to punch his head returned with a vengeance, as, purposely not seeing that she was gaping at his lofty reply, he turned, and had gone striding off in the direction which he had been going before she had called after him.

The light of battle had been in her eyes when it was time to go down to dinner, but only for her to be filled with impotent anger, for Zare had not put in an appearance at dinner. It had been from Anna-Maria that Laine had gleaned the information that the master was in his *studio*, Anna-Maria leaving her to guess that if he was eating dinner at all that night, then it would be served to him while he worked in his study.

Laine had tried very hard to be reasonable. She tried to cool her annoyance by acknowledging that since he must be spending hours at the hospital each day, then obviously his work was piling up. It was understandable that he should shut himself away in his study the minute he came home, she reasoned, his backlog of work had to be caught up on some time. And that he had no time to spare for so much as a few minutes in which to hear what she had to say had nothing to do with the feeling she was trying to squash that, not liking her, Zare Forturini would not spare time to listen to her even if he could.

Well, he wasn't at work in his study now, she thought, not feeling as generous with her reasoning that morning. Though nothing would get sorted, she thought as she left her room, if she went at it bull-at-a-gate fashion.

Not wanting another head-on collision of the aggression experienced on Tuesday when she had sailed out of the dining room having served her own backhanded version of an insult, Laine tried to keep calm as she entered the breakfast room and saw the man she wanted to see put down the newspaper he was reading and courteously rise.

Mollified slightly that, even though he disliked her, his good manners still prevailed, she took her seat and wished him a mild, 'Good morning, Zare.'

'Good morning to you, Laine,' he replied smoothly, a speculative look in his eyes to know what she was up to now as he resumed his seat but not his reading. Her mild manner, she guessed, hadn't fooled him for a second.

'May I?' she asked politely, her hand going to his

coffee-pot. Receiving his nod, still keeping calm, she poured herself a cup of coffee, her voice conversational as she enquired, 'You've telephoned the hospital this morning, of course?'

She knew he had got her. Knew that he had found out what lay behind her mild manner, owning, as a touch of arctic cold came to his voice as he replied, 'Of course,' that she had perhaps been about as subtle as a sledgehammer.

Hanging grimly on to her cool, Laine put down the coffee-pot and placed the cup she had just filled to the right of her. 'And how is Cristo this morning?' she asked, wanting for Cristo's sake that he should be better, but needing for her own sake that he should be improved so that she could return to England with an easy conscience.

'He—has had a restless night,' came her answer, a few more degrees of frost settling in, just as though, she thought, he thought it was her fault that his brother had slept badly!

About to get angry that having damned her, she would have all the sins in creation set at her door, Laine swallowed down her ire to stick in there grimly.

'Do I gather from that that Cristo is not being allowed to see anyone but family again today?'

Steady dark eyes met hers, an alertness in his that had her suspecting he had successfully read in her eyes what was in her mind. Though it was evenly that he replied:

'The hospital are being very strict about that rule.'

'Which must mean,' said Laine, trying her own hand at an insincere smile, 'that your brother has not resumed calling for me.' And not needing an answer, for had that been the case, Zare would have seen to it, whether the hospital agreed or not, that Cristo saw her, 'Which leaves me, Zare,' she said with another insincere smile, 'having to ask you to hand over my return ticket.'

'Return ticket, Laine?' he enquired, beating her at the insincere smile game, as he pretended not to know what she was talking about.

'I think you'll agree with me,' she said, only just managing to grab back temper as her cool front started to slip, 'that since I'm not going to be allowed to see him, I might as well go home.'

She was sure he must often have regretted his decision to bring her with him on Monday, and would speed her away with indecent haste. But having wondered countless times herself whatever she was doing there when each idle day passed with no sign of her being allowed to see Cristo passing with it, Laine's eyes started to go wide when, as if the penny had only just dropped—when she knew he was so sharp it was a wonder he didn't cut himself—Zare murmured softly:

'Ah, I see.' And while she was counting up to ten, regretfully he added, 'Would that it were possible to hand over your return ticket, *signorina*, but ...' he paused to offer her another insincere apology for a smile, '... unfortunately, I purchased your ticket for—one way only.'

That 'unfortunately' as, winded and trying not to show it she stared at him, told her he was tired of having her under his roof. But when nothing further came from him—no quick offer to rectify the situation and purchase a one-way ticket to England without further delay, coming either—a fierce pride rose up and took charge of Laine. That the man was a fiend of the first water went without saying. But because he thought she did not care from whom she took money, nothing on God's earth would have her asking him for her air fare home.

'Even though I don't like living in a foreign country without money,' she told him coldly, to let him know that not a twopenny piece towards her flight would she take from him, 'it would appear that I shall have to.'

To have her words interpreted to mean something she had not meant, as mockingly he questioned, 'You are still angling for me to pay you to stay?' left Laine with no hope whatsoever of hanging on to her temper.

'I wouldn't take so much as a half lira from you!' she flew, hot colour pinking her cheeks as she flared on, 'I haven't yet worked out how I'm going to get back to England when I don't have so much as the price of a stamp with me, but . . .'

On the instant she was chopped off. 'You have written to someone?' he barked, leaving her to stare at the sudden change in him from the mocking man he had been to this man who, from his jutting jaw apart from anything else, was now showing her that aggression which she did not need.

'No,' she snapped, 'I haven't written to anyone.'

'Not the boy-friend?' he charged hostilely.

'I said—no one,' Laine fired back—but then had to wonder at the abrupt changes in the man. For his voice was much less aggressive when he pressed, to have her faltering:

'Not even your parents?'

She looked away, remembering how she had been going to write to her parents when she arrived back home. She had thought, having seen Cristo by then, that she could tell them that not only had she been in Italy for a few days, but also that Cristo had been very ill but that he was now out of the wood. Her anger took a dive as, contrary to what she was certain the man sitting opposite was thinking—that she was a callous wretch who couldn't even be bothered to write to her parents—she felt sorely in need of seeing their kind unflappable faces right at this minute.

'My parents,' she replied at last, the fight going out of her in her need to feel the security of being part of a family again, 'will be in Australia by the time any letter I write reaches New Zealand.' That sounded double Dutch, she thought, though flicking a glance across the table, she saw Zare didn't look too puzzled. But mutiny was replaced by a sadness brought on by feeling the odd one out in more ways than one as she explained, 'I didn't bring my brother's address with me, so I can't write care of where he lives.'

'It makes you sad that you cannot correspond with your parents?'

Amazed that here again was a change in the man she had thought she was beginning to know, positive that she had heard a thread of kindness, of understanding of how she felt, in his voice, Laine looked up to see that for once there was no harshness in his expression.

'I . . .' she began, her voice coming through more huskily as she coped with a sensation of feeling choked up inside. 'I—didn't expect to still be in Italy,' she managed to finish.

'Nor in a foreign land at all, without money,' he said quietly—but brought her rapidly out of her amazed state when, while he kept his eyes on her face, his hand went to the inside of his jacket to extract his wallet.

'I don't want your money!' Her pride up in arms, she saw his wallet slip back out of her view as the words shot from her.

'What a contradiction you are,' he murmured thoughtfully.

'Because of your conviction that I couldn't wait to get my hands on the money your brother is supposed to have given me?' she challenged with some heat.

Knowing her challenge was about to be replied to, probably with a reminder of his equal conviction that Cristo would never lie to him, she saw Zare check what he had been about to hurl back at her. And just as suddenly, that charm she had seen that first morning in his country was coming out in full force.

'It is too sunny a morning for your beautiful eyes to know the cloud of being upset,' he said, making her gape. 'Angelina will be here with your breakfast in a moment', he added, as he left his seat and came round to her chair. She felt his fingers trail down the side of her face, and had still not recovered at the change in him, when he said, 'Eat well—and think kindly of me if you can.'

'You're going—out,' she gulped, trying to get over the tingling his touch gave her right down to her very toes. 'To Siena?' she asked, feeling something of a fool, for he went out at this time every morning.

'To Siena,' he agreed, but appeared in no hurry to get there, she thought when, as was usual at the end of most of their conversations, he did not stride arrogantly away.

'To see Cristo?' she questioned.

She saw his eyes shutter—to hide his emotions on being reminded of Cristo in his sickbed, she guessed. But suddenly she was rediscovering that sensitivity in her that did not want him to dwell on painful thoughts. And before he could tell her whether it was business or Cristo which took him to Siena, she was asking brightly:

'Can I come with you?'

His charm, she remembered, had not lasted long

that other time. And she could forget any idea that he
didn't like to see her eyes cloud over when he left her
upset, she saw. For he didn't care a damn whether he
upset her or not, she heard, as, thrusting the hand that
had trailed down her face into his pocket, aggression
back in full measure, he bit:

'You are so eager to see him, *signorina*, that you can
so easily forget I have told you he may see no one but
family?'

Her temper instant, retaliation to his aggression
instant, it was touch and go that she didn't answer him
in kind and for one or other of them to go storming
angrily off. But Laine's sensitivities having been
stirred by all that Zare must be going through, the
mental anguish he must be suffering over Cristo,
somehow she managed to hold down the hot words
that spurted to her lips. Though it was a shade tightly
that she told him:

'Very well, *signore*, I'll accept what you say, since I
must.' But her anger was still fighting with sensitivity
and a certain amount of heat was coming through, as
she told him bluntly, 'But if you think I'm going to sit
around here all day twiddling my thumbs, then do you
have another think coming!'

Not sure what she thought he would retaliate with—
most likely call her bluff and ask, since anywhere she
went would have to be on foot, where was it she was
thinking of going, she felt mutiny rear in her again.
But as she stared at him, enmity in her eyes, she saw
that his aggression was being tempered by an aloof
look as, managing to surprise her again, he asked:

'You have taken a dislike to my home?'

'Despite what you think of me,' she retorted, not
taking too kindly to that knack he had of never
answering in the way she expected, 'I *am* capable of

appreciating beauty when I see it!' His look of aloofness was beginning to fade, she noticed, but by then she was uncaring what expression he wore. 'But while I find your home, its setting, little short of idyllic,' she went on, 'I'm just *not* used to prolonged idleness. Anna-Maria,' she complained, 'won't even let me wash up so much as a tea-cup.'

'I have heard of your many offers of assistance,' he replied, his eyes steady on her mutinous face. 'Giuseppe,' he continued, humour lighting his face when Laine was thinking the situation far from funny, 'has told me he is wondering if he should lock up his gardening implements lest you purloin his favourite hoe.'

'I *do* know a weed from a flower,' she pointed out, aware by now that Giuseppe had a love affair going with the grounds and gardens he spent so many hours in.

'Please, *signorina*, I beg you,' said Zare, his mouth astonishingly picking up at the corners, no sign of the sour brute he had been about him, 'please whisper that word "weed".' And, charming her when she didn't want to be charmed, 'We don't want Giuseppe going into heart failure, do we?'

Despite herself, Laine had to smile, albeit she turned her face so that he should not see that the picture of Giuseppe clutching at his chest should a weed dare to show its head had amused her.

But her smile was not long in evidence. For, her eyes drawn back to him when she saw the movement of his hands go inside his jacket, she was at once ready with hot proud protests, when calmly he withdrew some notes and pushed them at her.

'I don't . . .' was as far as she got before, chopping her off in that manner she had grown used to, Zare successfully startled her into staring at him, when he said:

'I expect you will want the price of a cup of coffee while you take a look around Siena.'

'Siena!' The exclamation broke from her even as she saw that the notes that were somehow in her hand, though not enough for her air fare, were more than enough to treat herself to over a dozen cups of coffee.

'I have business there which will keep me busy until one—will you be all right on your own?'

'Can a duck swim?' she answered, a smile breaking at this surprise treat.

By the sound of it, even though she was not going to be allowed to go to the hospital with him, Zare was offering her a lift into that most beautiful of cities! But, anticipating that he had no further time to waste, he had been ready to depart five minutes ago, she recalled, she saw as those dark eyes stayed with her mouth that for once was curving in a natural smile, that he seemed to have forgotten that he had any urgency to do anything.

'Is—something the matter?' she asked, the question forced from her when he still had not moved.

His eyes pulled away from her mouth. 'Nothing that need trouble you,' he replied. 'I was thinking—that you had better call upstairs for a jacket.'

With the sun streaming through the windows, at any other time Laine might have argued with him. But, excitement taking charge of her, she was on her feet and halfway through the door. 'It's your climate,' she said over her shoulder. If Zare thought his Italian sun was not yet strong enough for her to go without a coat, so be it.

Reaching her room, she raced to the wardrobe, the sound of a vehicle starting up having her rocketing to the window. Her panic died when she saw Giuseppe at the wheel of the Land Rover, probably on another of his two-hour excursions, drive round the side of the house.

'You haven't yet had breakfast,' Zare was there to remind her when, lest he should take it into his head to go without her, jacket in hand, she fairly flew down the stairs and very nearly cannoned into him at the bottom.

Firm hands came to steady her, making her aware, from her rush she was sure, how energetically her heart was pumping.

'Who cares about breakfast?' she replied, a grin breaking so that the serious-eyed man who was looking levelly back at her just had to know that she could not wait to get to that city that centuries ago had been built on three hills.

Siena, Laine learned when Zare, not hanging about, passed Giuseppe and the Land Rover on the way, was not all that far distant from Valgaro. But on stopping the car to let her off in that ancient city, her excitement was to dip a little as she realised that by waiting for her, he had let her cut into the time he must want to spend with Cristo.

Though having stopped the car near the breathtaking white and dark green marble cathedral, Zare appeared in no hurry to be gone. For, coming round to the passenger side where she had already got out so as not to delay him further, he brought with him a street map which he must have collected when she had gone upstairs for her jacket.

'Any good with a street map?' he asked, looking to be going to open it up to show her exactly where they were.

'Brilliant,' lied Laine, taking it from him, conscious

as she was that to stay studying the map would cut further into his time.

She flicked him a glance from beneath her long lashes. And suddenly she was grinning again. Somehow she knew that he was aware of her lie. But she had no power to stop that grin, for as her heart began to pump energetically again, Laine saw that Zare was grinning too! This man who had a lion's share of aggression, was actually grinning at her, no aggression or bad temper to be seen that when he was such a stickler for the truth, she had lied to him.

'You can't get lost,' he murmured as he went back round to the driver's side of the car. 'I'll meet you back here at one.'

Standing to watch him drive off, Laine had to own, whether it be excitement, or what it was, even with Cristo still very ill, suddenly she was happy.

Her initial thought was to go inside the cathedral to have a look round. Then she thought that since it was near to the cathedral that she was to meet Zare, then perhaps it would be better to leave that until last, when if she had cut it a bit fine, she would be in the actual vicinity of where they were to meet. Turning her back on the cathedral, she set off to explore.

That morning turned out to be the most fascinating of morning in her whole twenty-two years. Through cobbled pavementless streets and alleys she went, and knowing nothing whatsoever about architecture, she was to stand transfixed staring at the Gothic buildings of the mediaeval city.

Once or twice as she went she had felt called to investigate a square she had seen through passageways. The next time that compulsion pulled, she obeyed it.

And it was there in the Piazza del Campo that, her breath taken, she just stood and looked and looked.

She was totally unaware of people, of pigeons, of souvenir sellers, her eyes drawn again and again to the tall stately rose-bricked Mangia Tower that stood guard at the Palazzo Pubblico. Her breath caught yet again as in the same magnificent shell-shaped piazza, the central point where the three hills met, by just turning her head she could see the beautiful curving Palazzo Sansedoni.

Laine could have stayed and spent the rest of the time at her disposal in just feasting her eyes on the magnificent Piazza del Campo. But on checking the one-handed clock on the Mangia Tower against her watch, she saw that time was going on, and that if she was to explore before she met Zare at one, then she hadn't a minute to waste.

Back in the charming streets and alleyways, Laine was content just to breathe in the atmosphere as she strolled past shops and paused occasionally to glance in shop windows. But it was when a small splash of yellow in the window of a shop selling glass and porcelain caught her eye that she stopped to do more than glance.

The splash of yellow that had attracted her attention turned out to be the most delicate small white china plate upon which, all around the edge, were sprigs of individually moulded yellow forsythia.

Lost in admiration, Laine gazed and gazed at the exquisite piece of porcelain and knew only she wanted, quite desperately, to be its owner. But, as minutes ticked by with nothing else in the window having any attraction for her, suddenly it was borne in on her exactly why she wanted that plate—the forsythia reminded her of that house at Valgaro, Zare's house!

With no idea of why she should want to take a memory she could touch with her back to England, a small sigh left her that everything in that window shrieked 'expensive' and Laine at last turned away.

Still trying to put the piece of porcelain from her mind, she checked her map only when she found herself in the Piazza Matteotti. A department store, its sunblinds advertising it as 'Upim', beckoned, but living with the one disappointment of her day that she could not afford that piece of porcelain, Laine decided against going inside for a quick look round. It wasn't that she needed to buy anything, but still mourning that even if she had more than her coffee money with her, that porcelain plate would still have been beyond her means, she thought she would prefer not to see anything else she could not afford.

Memory of her coffee money reminded her that she was thirsty. What better place to sit with a cup of coffee, she thought, a smile beginning, than the Piazza del Campo! There had been tables and chairs galore set outside the various restaurants there, she recalled, banishing disappointment that she would never own that particular piece of porcelain as she retraced her steps, eager now to return to that one particular square.

Of course, only human, she could not resist another look at the small plate as she passed the window. But telling herself that a cup of coffee in the Piazza del Campo was one very big compensation, she went on and was soon, once more, lost to time as her ears picked up the sound of multi-national voices, with yet no particular language able to penetrate her rapture.

Quite when she realised how sublimely content she felt just to sit there amongst the strange echoing quality of sound that came back from the walls, Laine did not know. Nor did she know for how long she had sat there. Spellbound, she was unaware that her coffee cup had long since been empty, and she had room only for happiness.

Her enthralled trance was only broken when a shadow fell across her, and she became aware that the sun had become temporarily hidden. But when she looked up and saw that it was Zare Forturini who, standing looking down at her, was responsible for the shadow, still bewitched, she felt neither surprise nor discomfort that he had had to come looking for her.

The scene fixed in her mind, Zare seemed all part and parcel of the whole wonderful feel of it all. Her eyes shining, the most beautiful smile broke from her to reveal her enchantment, as, any formal greeting passing her by, she sighed:

'Isn't it all so . . . so absolutely marvellous!'

But to find that Zare was looking at her a shade oddly, that he wasn't saying anything at all, had it suddenly penetrating that, as ever polite with her in company, he was probably furious that he had had to come and find her, yet with the area abounding with tourists, he was waiting to let fly at her until they were alone.

'Er—is it one o'clock already?' she asked, a hint of apology in her voice as she waited for some tight-lipped reply.

He did speak then, and all at once all was well with her world again, and her heart lifted when he smiled, and asked:

'You have enjoyed yourself so much that you forgot all sense of time?'

'It's been the most wonderful morning of my life,' she told him honestly, her smile there again as her eyes, leaving his, just had to do another circuit of the piazza. 'Was there ever such a place?' she asked softly.

To feel his hand on hers, cool, yet oddly warm as he

pulled her to her feet and placed a note on top of the
bill for her coffee, had a tingling shooting up her arm,
and for a moment Laine felt quite giddy. Though
later she was able to realise that that was no more than
should be expected when taking into account that she
had had no breakfast, had walked around for hours,
and that her senses had been assaulted by beauty after
beauty.

Feeling an apology was due to him, she was still in
her enraptured world, yet another smile of happiness
breaking from her when, his hand still holding hers,
Zare sounded as if he was apologising to her when he
looked deep into her eyes and said softly:

'Loath though I am to be the one to break the spell
il Campo has on you, Anna-Maria will be waiting to
serve you lunch.'

Here's a sweetheart of an offer!

Take these **4 FREE ROMANCE NOVELS,** plus a **FREE TOTE BAG,** with no obligation to buy!

Say Hello to Yesterday

Holly Weston had raised her small son and worked her way up to features writer for a major newspaper.

She had been very young when she married Nick Falconer—but old enough to lose her heart completely when he left. Despite her success in her new life, her old one haunted her.

But it was over and done with—until an assignment in Greece brought her face to face with Nick, and all she was trying to forget …

Man's World

Kate's new boss, editor Eliot Holman, might have devastating charms—but Kate couldn't care less, even if he was interested in her.

Everyone, including Eliot, thought Kate was grieving over the loss of her husband, Toby. She kept it a secret just how cruelly Toby had treated her and how terrified she was of trusting men again.

But Eliot refused to leave her alone. He was no different from other men … or was he?

Born Out of Love

Charlotte stared at the man through a mist of confusion. It was Logan. An older Logan, of course, but unmistakably the man who had ravaged her emotions and then abandoned her all those years ago.

She ought to feel angry. She ought to feel resentful and cheated. Instead, she was apprehensive—terrified at the complications he could create …

Time of the Temptress

Rebellion against a cushioned, controlled life had landed Eve Tarrant in Africa. Now only the tough mercenary Wade O'Mara stood between her and possible death in the wild, revolution-torn jungle.

But the real danger was Wade himself—he had made Eve aware of herself as a woman …

Your Four Free Harlequin Novels will take you to a world of romance, love and desire. If you choose become a Harlequin Home Subscriber, you'll be le to indulge in romantic adventure again and again th new novels every month. Experience the world Harlequin by returning the reply card below. u'll receive your 4 FREE BOOKS, FREE TOTE and YSTERY GIFT. Mail your card today!

Take these 4 books and tote bag FREE!

Affix the special heart here and we'll also send you a special Mystery Gift!

Mail to Harlequin Reader Service
2504 W. Southern Ave., Tempe, AZ 85282

Yes, please send me FREE and without obligation my 4 Harlequin Presents novels. If you do not hear from me, please send me 6 new Harlequin Presents novels each month as soon as they come off the presses. I understand that I will be billed only $10.50 for all 6 books. There are no shipping and handling nor any other hidden charges. There is no minimum number of books that I have to purchase. In fact, I can cancel this arrangement at any time. The 4 books, tote bag, and mystery gift are mine to keep as FREE gifts, even if I do not buy any additional books.

106 CIP BA5M

Name	(please print)	
Address		Apt. No.
City	State	Zip

Signature (if under 18, parent or guardian must sign)

This offer is limited to one order per household and not valid to present subscribers. We reserve the right to exercise discretion in granting membership. Prices subject to change.

Affix special Heart on reply card to receive your Mystery Gift

CHAPTER SIX

CAPTIVATED, as she had been since she had first set foot in Siena, Laine was to find, as she got ready to go down to dinner that night, that she still felt bewitched, not only by Siena, but by everything at Valgaro too.

That Zare Forturini must have something to do with her inner contentment, when all the odds were against her experiencing a moment's contentment, was, she had to own, strangely true. For had he returned to being the uncivil brute she had thought he might be once they were away from other people, then her joy with anything his country held would, she knew, be shattered. Back then would come the nagging worries of being penniless in a land that was not her own, of having to live in a house where aggression between her and her host was never very far from the surface. And back would come her anxiety about the poor progress Cristo was making.

With a start, she realised that, as completely had she forgotten all about the bad temper that had flared between her and Zare at breakfast time, so too had she forgotten to ask him how Cristo had been when he had visited him that morning!

Wondering how she could have forgotten such a thing, Laine recalled that she had had plenty of opportunity to ask Zare how his brother was. For, expecting when he had brought her back that he would stay no longer than to drop her off, she had been surprised that for the first time while she had been there, he had eaten lunch at home.

A trace of a smile curving her mouth, Laine met her shining eyes in the mirror as she completed her light make-up. Some self-defence mechanism made her ask, why shouldn't her eyes shine? Zare had been at his most charming at lunchtime, not a glimmer of his mighty aggression coming through as, having almost to drag her away from *il Campo*, he had seen that she was still glowing from all that her eyes had seen.

His teasing comment when seated opposite her at lunch of, 'Have you yet come down to earth?' had seen the gates opening on a multitude of questions that had tumbled to her lips.

That he indulged her by answering every one of her questions, bringing to life in answer to her question about the many gaily coloured banners she had seen on sale everywhere, that they were the flags of the seventeen Sienese districts, and were much in evidence when twice a year, once in July and once in August, a horse race called the *Palio* was run in *il Campo*. His description of how the crowd went wild when, with only ten districts allowed to compete, the ten horses with their saddleless riders raced three times round the Campo, was so vivid that it was all she could do to hold back from saying, 'Oh, how I wish I could be here to see it!'

Leaving her seat at the dressing table, her mind still full of all that Zare had told her, Laine brought herself up short as the realisation suddenly came of just how much space Zare Forturini too had occupied in her thoughts since that amicable lunch.

But she was to stand rooted in the middle of her bedroom floor, when with something akin to shock, she realised, when at one time she had thought him the most hateful man she had ever met, that she did not hate him at all! So much did she not hate him—she had even forgotten her usual thought when she had heard his car return, of 'Oh God—he's back'!

Deciding some minutes later that perhaps it was only natural her hate would not stand up now that she had been treated to an hour of his warmer side, Laine left her room with the shine in her eyes dimmed as she guessed that, since Zare's charm only came in short bursts, she would most likely be back to hating him by the time dinner was over. For at the first opportunity she intended to rectify her omission in not asking how Cristo was and, if memory served, only seconds after Cristo was brought into any conversation, firing pins were put into position with both of them ready to let fly.

But when Zare came into the *sala* where, a few minutes early, she was sitting, and she discovered that he had retained that charm she had decided appeared only in short bursts, as he remarked, 'I thought I heard you,' and, although he was unsmiling, looked as though he was pleased to see her, all thought of her enquiry about Cristo went from her.

And she was busy with thoughts, as he escorted her in to dinner, of, had he really looked pleased to see her sitting there? Or had she imagined it? And why should it bother her anyway? It was not until much later that thoughts of Cristo entered her head.

'You were not—too bored, this afternoon?' he enquired as the meal progressed, remembering, she thought, that she had told him she was not used to idleness.

'Not bored at all,' she told him politely as she cut into some pork cooked in a superb wine sauce. 'How could I be?' she questioned in return. And her mouth curved warmly as she remembered and did not wait for his answer. 'I spent hours in the garden, just thinking and thinking.'

'Your thoughts obviously gave you pleasure,' he stated, his eyes going to the curve of her mouth, then up to her eyes.

She guessed, one's thoughts being private, that that was the nearest he would go to ask her what she had been thinking about. But that he was interested at all in any of what she had been thinking made her feel oddly pleased with life.

'Can't you remember the first time you saw Siena?' she asked.

'Ah,' he said, and she knew that her question had revealed to him where her thoughts had been that afternoon. 'So you have not forgotten this place that brings stars to your eyes,' he said softly.

'I never shall,' she murmured, remembering again the Piazza del Campo, that echoing sound she had heard in her ears again whenever she thought about the place where she had sat, regardless of time ticking by, and sipped her coffee. 'And that reminds me,' she said, having to explain the thoughts that were going through her head as she laid down her knife and fork and rooted in her bag. 'I was just thinking of the Campo where I had coffee. I forgot to return the money you gave me.'

His eyes flicked to the notes she was trying to hand him, and then back to her face, his look steady as he remarked, 'You do not appear to have spent very much.'

'I didn't spend any of it,' she replied, trying not to get uptight as it came to her that with the opinion he had of her, he no doubt thought it peculiar that she was offering him his money back at all, much less that she hadn't made a hole in it. 'If you remember,' she added with a touch of heat, 'it was you who settled the bill for my coffee.'

'So I did,' he replied. And as if he could see she was going to blow up if he didn't take the money she was pushing at him, he took it from her, that steady look being relieved by a hint of a smile, as he said, 'Your memory is much better than mine, Laine.'

'Now who's telling fibs?' she asked, and thought she had said the wrong thing again when, at being accused of being a liar, his face fell back into stern lines. 'I was only joking,' she said quickly, half of her wondering why she was bothering to try to placate him, while the other half of her was glad that it had worked, for that half smile was back there again. But she did not press what she knew to be the truth—that Zare Forturini never forgot a thing, because, his good humour restored, he was asking:

'Did you see nothing that you wanted to buy?'

Instantly her mind went to the porcelain plate she had seen, and the memory of it caused her to hesitate before, knowing the plate was lost to her for ever, she told him:

'I didn't go into any shops. I saw Upim, of course, and a shop that sold some delicious-looking cake— *panforte*, I think it was called.'

'The cake of Siena,' Zare told her, going on to let her know they were talking about the same one by saying it was, with variations, made from flour, candied peel, melon and citrus, almonds and sugar. 'Anna-Maria will make some for you,' he ended. And before she could protest that she didn't want Anna-Maria to be put to any trouble, he was going on, 'Are you going to tell me what it was you saw, wanted, but did not buy?'

Surprise had her jaw dropping. 'How did you

kn . . .' His grin, her thoughts scattering as her
heart doing a quick flip as she observed it, made her
break off.

At that moment Anna-Maria came in to see if they
had finished, and looking down, Laine saw that she
had placed her knife and fork neatly side by side on
her empty plate without knowing it.

Too full for more than a piece of fruit to end with,
she realised that they had almost completed another
meal without either of them going for the other's
throat. Perhaps Zare has been trying to hold back in
the same way I have, she thought, and found that that
thought pleased her. But mindful that it only took a
little spark to set one or other of them off, as Anna-
Maria finished tidying the dining room table, then
went out, Laine thought she would stay just long
enough to finish the apple Zare had peeled for her,
then she would return to her room.

'You did not answer my question.'

Zare's statement took her attention from the last two
pieces of apple. She knew what his question had been,
but still not wanting that spark to arc, she could not,
since he valued honesty so much, pretend that she
didn't.

Though it was still a mystery to her why she should
want a tangible memory with her when she returned to
England, Laine began to tell him about the porcelain
plate. But, too concerned with hoping he would not
see the connection with his home, she was unaware
that in her description of the forsythia-decorated
object, she had revealed how instantly she had fallen
in love with it. That was, until he said:

'You wanted that plate very badly, did you not,
Laine? I should have given you more mon . . .'

'No!' she interrupted him sharply—but had to add,

when he looked at her with slightly raised brows, 'Even if you had, I would never have spent your money on a present for myself.'

She knew her colour was high. Knew that with Zare staring at her it was never likely to recede. Just as she knew that the reason for her warm colour was because he was thinking that the price of a piece of porcelain was neither here nor there when he had written proof that she had accepted more than the outlay for a piece of porcelain from his brother.

Unable to bear his scrutiny any more, Laine pushed her chair back from the table. 'If you'll excuse me,' she said, 'I think I'd better go to my room.'

To find him at the door before she could get to it was unexpected. And just as unexpected was the fact that when she thought he would open the door for her to go through, Zare did no such thing.

'You do not sound—too sure—that you want to go to your room,' he suggested, when she looked at him questioningly.

Sighing, Laine saw that a lengthy and probably fiery argument might ensue if she didn't come clean. 'I've had a lovely day, Zare,' she told him honestly. 'But quite frankly, I can sense both my temper—and your temper—wearing thin. And . . .'

'And,' he took up, 'you would prefer that your day will stay lovely until, with your head on your pillow, you close your eyes?'

'I—couldn't have . . .' Suddenly, at the warm look that came to his eyes, seeing it mattered not to him, she was sure, how her day ended, Laine felt choked up inside. '. . . couldn't have put it better myself,' she managed to finish, finding she was glad her voice was naturally husky.

'Then with the hope that I shall not be the one to

spoil your lovely day, may I say goodnight as a—
friend and, for once, not your enemy,' he said softly,
that warm look for her still in his eyes, as giving her all
the time she needed to pull away if she had any
objection, gently Zare Forturini took her in his arms.

Too confused suddenly to know if this was the
way in which friends parted, Laine had no objection
to make whatsoever when he laid his mouth over
hers. In fact, so little objection did she have to make
that when, his kiss still gentle, his mouth stayed over
hers, she found that her hands were going up to his
shoulders.

Her heart drumming inside her, she felt warmth in
his kiss; felt the warmth of him as he held her close in
the circle of his arms.

Then, just when she had ceased thinking about
anything at all in particular, she felt Zare, unhurried
still, gently push her from him.

His smile had gone, and her colour had pinkened a
little, when with his eyes still holding hers, Zare
opened the door and moved her a little way to it.

'I think the idea of you going to your room is a good
one,' he said slowly, while all she was capable of doing
was to look at him. 'But I think you had better not—
delay any longer.'

As a help to reduce her pink colour, his remark was
of no help. Was he saying that he—desired her? That
if she did not go now, that he would not be able to let
her go at all?

'G-goodnight,' she stammered, owning the oddest
compulsion to stay just where she was to find out
exactly what it was he did mean.

'Goodnight, Laine,' floated after her.

And Laine was doing some floating herself as,
suspecting his eyes were following her since she had

not heard the dining room door close, she went without a backward glance up the stairs.

Only when she had made it to her room did her heart decide to behave itself. Though it threatened to go erratic as she thought of how that kiss, as lovely as her day, had been. But it was not until she opened her eyes to another new day that it came to her that not once last night had she asked Zare how his brother was!

He must be showing signs of improvement by now, she thought—not that she knew a lot about illness. But it was almost a week since he had been taken back to hospital. And surely if his condition was going the other way, then given, as Zare had said, that Anna-Maria was always singing, that news would have seen her singing something other than the snatches of the merry tunes she frequently broke into.

Thinking that perhaps today would be the day she would be allowed to see the man who, after all, was the sole reason for her being there, Laine felt an unexpected shyness attack her when she left her room to go down to breakfast.

Yesterday had been little short of wonderful, she thought, as, wondering if Zare worked on Saturdays, that shyness made her footsteps slower than usual as she went down the stairs.

Memory of that kiss she had shared with him last night was with her as she crossed the hall floor. Excitement and shyness mingled together as she guessed that the antagonism between her and Zare, despite her being unable to disprove any of what he had first thought of her, would never again surface. For her part, with that beautiful warm kiss between them, she would find it impossible to get cross with him about anything.

Or so she thought before she opened the door to the breakfast room. Shyly she smiled at the man who, on hearing the door open, took his eyes from his paper, and the good manners inherent in him made him stand up until she had taken her place at the table, her husky, 'Good morning, Zare,' leaving her as suddenly needing some action, she immediately picked up her serviette.

But her serviette was to go promptly down on to her side plate when, not replying to her greeting, his tone curt, telling her that it had not taken him long to regret having said 'goodnight' as a friend, he remarked shortly:

'You went to bed with your appetite not satisfied, *signorina*?' And smoothly, while she sat stunned, 'It is no wonder that you cannot wait to begin breakfast this morning!'

Dumbfounded at the change in him, at the difference in him from what she had been expecting, Laine heard him summoning Angelina to bring her breakfast, while her thoughts went whirling at what he had just said. Ignoring the fact that she thought she had read desire in his eyes last night, and brushing aside that although she knew he could have read a similar look in her eyes; last night they had exchanged a warm kiss that had banished, or so in her innocence she had thought, all the animosity that had been between them. Last night she had been foolish enough to think that that kiss had set a seal on a new beginning. A new beginning, if maybe not exactly as friends, then certainly not as enemies.

Still trying to come to terms with the fact that last night she had been Laine, but that since Zare had gone to bed and obviously thought over all he knew of her—none of it good, she could be positive of that—he had decided the distance of calling her *signorina* more fitting, Laine was never more glad of the fierce pride which had been handed down to her by both her proud parents. It was all she had to save her from showing weak tears at the slap in the face she had just received.

Angelina bustling in with her coffee and toast gave her a minute or two to do what she could to get herself together. But as Angelina went out, Laine had caught her second wind, and attacked without thought that when it came to a battle of words, Zare was not backward when it came to cutting her down to size.

'Forgive me, *signore*,' she said coolly, 'but I think I really should tell you that when I went to bed last night, it was without wanting a single thing more you could supply to ensure my satisfaction. Though,' she added, ignoring the narrowing of his eyes as off came the gloves and from somewhere she dredged up an insincere smile, 'from the grumpy way you're behaving this pleasant morning, I should say, of the two of us, that you're the one suffering from—er—night starvation, not I.'

She knew her cheeks were warm as she brought out that last bit. Guessed that Zare knew she was nowhere near as cool as she was making out to be, but pride riding her, she would not back down, as her head tilted as arrogantly as his ever had done and she watched as, grim-faced, he studied her.

'Perhaps you in turn will forgive me, *signorina*,' he said, his voice silky when, his inspection of her over, he at last spoke, 'in that I must correct the erroneous impression you have that I am starving for anything.' His smile beat hers into a cocked hat when it came to insincerity. And it was then, his voice hardened, his eyes going like chips of ice, as he told her cuttingly, loathing her and all she stood for, she knew it, 'My needs are amply provided for without my having to—degrade myself by—without too much effort—gaining access to your bed.'

Her colour flared crimson, hurt she could not hide in her eyes as she tried to remain proud. But she felt whipped by what he had said, and it was a toss-up then, as her jaw wavered as she pulled in a gasp of that hurt, whether she would have taken to her heels and run from the room. But as pride battled in her to stay put, to make believe he had not cut her to the quick, so, as if he could not bear to look at her any longer, she heard the scrape of his chair, then saw him go striding from the room.

It was pride that he had had a good go at breaking that got Laine through the rest of the day. That he did not come home to lunch was a bonus she was grateful for. For no way would she sit at his table with him and eat so much as one morsel.

Insolent swine! she fumed on more than one occasion, back to hating him with all she had that even the enchantment she had always found in the garden was gone.

Oh, if only she had the money to get back to England, she thought impotently, her hate against Cristo's brother not letting up when the excuse tried to creep in that perhaps Cristo was worse this morning. Nothing would excuse the way Zare had spoken to her. Nothing would excuse what he had said, even if she had fired his wrath by getting in first to look down her nose at him for a change. And anyway, Anna-Maria had been singing like a wound-up canary the last time she had been anywhere near the kitchen, so at the very least, Cristo had to be holding his own.

Still mutinous, Laine was in her room when she heard Zare's car return. But by then, pride and mutiny combined were giving her second thoughts about not eating another morsel with him as a mealtime companion. He'd just love that, wouldn't he? she thought. He'd just love to think he'd made short work of her, with his talk of not degrading himself. He'd just love it if he thought she was skulking in her room licking the wounds he had inflicted.

Damn him, stormed her pride, she wouldn't buckle under his insults, she'd be hanged if she would!

Pride, Laine was to discover, was all very well, but it was no help to stop her hands from shaking as she zipped up her blue dress.

Accepting that she felt nervous, though whether of Zare having something equally delightful to snarl at her as the remark he had cut her with that morning, or from his astonishment that she was coming back for more, it was that stubborn pride that had her leaving her room at just gone half past eight.

Her head held high, she decided to go straight to the dining room. For pride's sake she had made it this far, but nerves were grabbing at her, and she just did not trust herself not to ruin her dignified front by throwing at him anything good manners decreed he offered her if she joined him in the *sala*, and he went off on the same tack he had been on from the very first that morning.

But on opening the dining room door, Laine was to find she had been mistaken to think that Zare was in the *sala*. For he was standing with his back to her over by the foreplace, tension, she could have sworn, about those broad shoulders the moment before he spun round and saw her there.

Not intending to give him any sort of greeting, since

he had seen fit to ignore her greeting of that morning, she moved to go over to her usual seat, and found that he had moved too, and was pulling out her chair for her.

Sure it was only from habit of upbringing that he had performed this service for her, Laine declined to thank him lest, since not one word had so far been exchanged, his mood was as brutish as it had been.

But, when she had thought that as far as she was concerned not one word would she utter, the better to keep her dignified air, it was as Zare went round to take his seat that, as her eyes went down, she observed the small parcel in an expensive-looking wrapping that was to the right of her place setting.

'What's this?' The words had left her involuntarily, too late now to bring them back, or to ignore the parcel as though she had never seen it.

'Why not unwrap it and find out?'

Aggression was absent from his voice, she noted, but that didn't mean it would not come roaring to the surface at the slightest pretext.

'You'll forgive me—I'd rather not,' she replied coldly, and wished that Anna-Maria, Angelina, or anybody would hurry in, because she was nervous of Zare Forturini who, ever a one with surprises, had changed tack yet again, and with her soup in front of her, it would give her some action to perform.

'It is *your* forgiveness I'm after, Laine,' said Zare, when her fingers refused to carry out his suggestion to open the package. 'My words to you this morning were unforgivable, I know, but . . .'

That the great Zare Forturini seemed, if her ears were not playing her false, to be apologising, made Laine raise her head to look at him, that choked-up feeling visiting her again when she could see no harshness for her in his expression.

'You think that forgiveness for your foul remark can be bought by a mere trinket?' she questioned, knowing she was needling him, but unable to sit there and meekly accept his gift.

'I hurt you,' he replied, to surprise her yet again when she thought that something short and sharp was going to come her way. 'And in truth,' he went on, 'I can't honestly say if that was my intention or not. But what I can honestly say is that seeing that hurt in your eyes has not made this day any easier to bear.'

Cristo! she thought, but could not then ask about him. She sensed that the news about Cristo that morning was not good, and she had been the one Zare had chosen to take his aggression out on at the impotency of being able to do no more than to get the best doctors he could to attend Cristo. But, having seen how his remarks had cut, he had had that to live with throughout that day as well as his fears about his brother.

'You had no need to—to buy me a present,' she said huskily. Having vowed never to forgive him, she realised that vow was as nothing when she saw how it had been.

'I did not buy it because I had to, Laine,' he told her quietly, 'but because I—wanted to.' He smiled at her then, the warm natural smile she had seen yesterday.

It was the same smile, yet as her heart started to bump painfully inside her as his eyes stayed with her, as she looked into those warm dark eyes, Laine's senses were revealing to her what had been there yesterday and probably the day before, only she had not seen it then.

Astonishment hit her like a body blow, and she was only barely aware that Anna-Maria had come in with a soup tureen, that she was being served with soup.

'*Grazie*, Anna-Maria,' she murmured, her voice barely audible as she tried to surface from shock. Tried to surface because she knew that she had to.

'Which are you going to do first?' Zare asked the moment the door had closed behind Anna-Maria. 'Open your parcel or drink your soup?'

Unable to answer him, or even look at him, Laine reached for the packet. Her fingers all thumbs, she pulled aside the gold tape and undid first the outer wrapper and then the swathe of tissue beneath. Then tears were jerking to her eyes.

'Oh—Zare!' she breathed. 'Oh Zare,' she choked, 'it's—beautiful!'

For there in her hands was the porcelain she had so admired yesterday. The porcelain plate she had wanted because her heart had known what she had only just discovered; that she had to have a reminder of this enchanted place. That, because she was in love with him, she had to have a reminder of Zare. And yet it could not be hers—it was far too expensive.

'It's beautiful,' she said again. 'But I can't . . .'

'You're not going to cry, are you?' she heard him cut in as tears shimmered in her eyes.

'As if I would,' she replied, and hoped he would think it was just the beauty of the object in her hands that was making her swallow hard lest her tears should fall.

Managing to check her tears, she looked at him. He was unsmiling, she saw, until she found a smile that told him she was not going to flood the place. Then, his mouth curving slightly, it was sincerely, she thought, that he said, 'It seems I have found the right piece—please accept it, Laine.'

She guessed from that that on top of all his worries that day, he had had to search until he had found the

piece she had described to him. And that made it even
more valuable to her—that Zare had gone out of his
way to get it for her.

'Thank you,' she heard herself murmur, and just
had to let him know that she understood. 'It's no
wonder you were a little touchy this morning,' she
said, smiling as she spoke, 'the way things are . . .'

'What the hell do you mean by that!' hit her before
she could blink.

Oh God, Laine thought, wondering what she had
done now to set him off. She wanted to beg him not to
spoil this wonderful moment for her. This moment of
his giving, of her taking because she loved him. Giving
and taking, she thought, and remembered her mother
saying that there had to be give and take if people were
going to get on.

'What would I mean, Zare?' she asked quietly, not
wanting his frown, wanting his smile back. 'I know
how worried you are about Cristo. The sort of strain
you've been under about him is enough to make
anyone touchy.'

'I am—a little on edge,' he owned, but miraculously
his frown had disappeared, as he added, 'Your soup is
getting cold.'

Despite the terrifying moment when Laine had
thought that at the very least she would be throwing
her beautiful plate back at him, to her great joy, his
aggression did not show itself throughout the
remainder of that meal.

Indeed, it seemed that Zare was trying hard to make
amends for the way he had been with her that
morning. For he had her chuckling several times with
his wit and humour. And Laine, already sunk, knew
she had no chance of being sensible and going straight
to her room as she should when, the meal at an end,

the china plate he had given her in her bag, when charmed by him as she had been, he suggested that they adjourn to the *sala*.

It was in the *sala* when, shyness again attacking, her source of conversation dried up, that all she could think to say as Zare drew up a chair very near to hers was:

'How was Cristo when you saw him today?'

She waited for his aggression to appear, biting her tongue at her question, although it was a natural one. Then discovered that for once his aggression was staying down when Cristo's name cropped up. And given that he took his time before replying, memory of his sick brother causing him to get up and pour himself a Scotch, his back was to her as he replied evenly:

'He was a little better when I saw him this afternoon.'

He came back with his Scotch, and a sherry for her. And Laine, glad in her heart that there was at last some improvement in Cristo, a crisis having taken place in the early hours of that morning, she guessed, saw that this was the reason for Zare's improved humour.

'Is he allowed to see anyone but family yet?' she felt emboldened enough to ask.

'You are anxious to see him?'

Was there a strain of aggression there? she wondered, desperately trying to remember the 'give' side of this give-and-take business.

'I thought,' she compromised at last, not wanting a fight, sorely needing when she went to bed that night to have the comfort of an aggressionless parting between them to help her through what she knew was going to be a wakeful night, 'I thought it was Cristo who was anxious to see me.'

'He is—in love with you?'

Oh lord, that frown was there again. 'No, I'm sure he isn't,' she replied, finding it harder to give than she would have thought at his doubting look. But pride was insisting on being heard when for once she would rather it stayed quiet. 'If you're thinking that it's odd he should give me two thousand pounds when he's not in love with me, then I can only repeat—he never gave me any money.'

That Zare had gone from her and was thinking his own thoughts told Laine that bed was the best place for her.

The sherry he had given her, she set down on a table beside her. But when she got to her feet, Zare stood too, that frown still with him as he asked:

'Where are you going?'

'To my room,' she replied, a woodenness in her voice that wouldn't be denied, no matter how much she did not want it there.

'But you haven't finished your drink yet.'

'I don't want a drink,' she told him, her voice quiet. 'And neither do I want a row with you. But with you unable to believe a word I say since Cristo has never, so you said, lied to you . . .'

'It is out of his character to lie to me,' he told her stiffly. 'Many times in the past I have given him a cheque when he has needed it, but never, even when he has known in advance that I will not like the project he required the money for, has he ever lied to me.'

To her mind, then, there seemed little more to be said. 'Goodnight, Zare,' she said, and would, she thought, have brushed past him to the door.

But, 'No, Laine,' broke from him, his hand coming to her arm to stay her, his action causing her to look at him. And she saw then that if a battle had been going on inside him about whom he should believe, her who he had known for less than a week, or the brother who had never lied to him, then since she was there and Cristo was not, with no way to get at the truth, Zare had, for the moment, grown weary of the subject. 'Don't go—not yet,' he said, when, her arm tingling from his touch, Laine found she just did not want to pull away.

It was her movement, she was sure afterwards, when she was teetering on the brink of knowing she would be wrong to stay for just a moment longer, when pride tugged her one way and instinct another, it was she who made that small movement towards him.

That movement was all that it needed. All that it needed for Zare to know the proud look of her was giving in to him, to the wish she had stated not to want to row with him.

And it was within a split second of her moving that he moved too. Moved to take her into his arms, to enfold her, to say not one word, but just to hold her quiet like that.

In his arms was where Laine wanted to be. To her it was heaven just to lean against him. Even not knowing what he wanted of her, she could not deny her need to be at peace with him.

For how long they stood like that in quiet harmony, she never knew, as in the circle of his arms she stayed and just wallowed in this chance to be close to him.

When she felt his hand at her hair, that hand seemed to be caressing, and she just had to look at him to see if the gentleness she felt emanating from him was real, or if it was only her imagination.

It was real, she saw, when she tilted her head back and gazed into dark eyes that looked back, then travelled her face from her clear brow, down past her eyes, her nose, her mouth, to her chin and back up to her mouth again. And it was then, when his eyes returned to her inviting lips, that some word of Italian escaped him, escaped him as though he had no memory of saying anything. Then, 'Laine,' he said, and the next moment his mouth was over hers.

And Laine gloried in the feel of his mouth on hers. Gloried to feel, as his hand left her hair, how he gathered her to him to hold her yet closer as, having no mind to do any other, her arms crept around him.

How long they stayed like that, holding each other, returning each kiss with a growing fire, Zare's mouth seeking her throat, her ears, as closer still he held her, Laine neither knew nor cared. She was oblivious to anything save that in Zare's arms was where she wanted to be. His mouth over hers, his body pressing hers, was what she wanted.

When he guided her to the couch, their movements mingling as one, the heady pleasure of what he was doing to her made her eyes close. She felt his hands at the fastenings of her clothes, and his touch was too much to bear without calling out his name.

'Zare,' she moaned at the feel of his hands on her naked breasts. She clutched on to him when with a sensual touch his fingers invited their pink tips into throbbing peaks, then in turn, he kissed both crowns.

Without conscious thought she knew that this night would see her his. It was what she wanted. And maybe because of all the hatred that had been between them, she wanted him to know that there was no longer hatred in her heart, that when she gave herself to him, it would be willingly. There was no thought in her of holding back—why should she want to, she loved him!

'Zare!' she cried his name again when his hands at her spine pressed her against him, his need for her waiting, that same yearning in him, she knew it.

'You want me, Laine?' he asked, his question not necessary as her arms about him she pressed nearer. Her legs entangling with his, she felt a thrill of wanting as he moved and lay with his weight over her. Her breath caught, a touch of unsuspected panic taking her as a groan left him and she knew she had stirred this vibrant male.

'Oh yes,' she breathed. 'Yes, Zare, I want you. I want you,' she sighed, her breath fading as his mouth cut off more words.

She knew then that be it here, or up in her room, wherever he chose to make her his would be right. And she knew it would be now, for Zare was helping her to sit up, his face flushed as she knew hers was, a furnace burning in his eyes as he gazed ardently at her uncovered breasts. By his action in bringing her to sit up, she knew it would be to an upstairs room that he would be taking her, but whether it was his room or hers mattered little to her.

And then, when his head came forward, and it seemed that he would just have to kiss her again before he took her anywhere, suddenly there was a sound outside. A sound, a car's engine warned him, just as it warned her, that they were about to have company.

Wanting to cry out, not wanting any interruption at this moment of all moments, she saw that already Zare was straightening her clothes. Wildly she wanted to tell him to lock the doors, not to let anyone in, for the way she was, still clinging to the slopes of the heights of desire he had taken her to, she thought it would be an age before she would be capable of going through the courtesies if whoever had arrived was to be introduced to her.

Her eyes searching his, she saw that furnace of wanting dim, saw that his face had fallen into stern lines. And she was undecided then as, her own clothes straightened, Zare set about buttoning up his shirt, whether he had recognised who had arrived from the sound of the car's engine and had no wish to see his visitor, or if he, like her, was damning the fact that anyone else knew where he lived.

Masculine footsteps coming along the hall had Zare standing in front of her to shield her as she strove to come back to normality, she guessed.

Her colour still high, she heard the door to the *sala* open, and knew then that she had only seconds to get herself somewhere back to normal. Though she could not help but feel a thrill at Zare's tone, for it was stern and not very welcoming to whoever it was who had called, for even as he reverted to his native Italian, she could hear that in his voice.

Italian was the language that answered him. Italian, and not at all put out at the aggressive greeting that he had got for his trouble. But it was not that that had Laine's eyes shooting wide! For even though not a word of that quick flow of foreign language was she able to understand, what her ears did pick up was some inflection in that answering voice with which she was very familiar. Somewhere she had heard that voice before!

Curiosity was to mingle with that feeling that perhaps it was about time she let the other man know there was someone else in the room.

Getting to her feet, Laine moved round to the side of where Zare had been shielding her. But as her eyes looked at the face of the man who had just come in, his face starting to register the same astonishment that was rocketing through Laine as he saw her, her eyes were telling her that indeed she did know him! And not only that, but that he was looking much better than the last time she had seen him. In fact, because there was nothing wrong with her eyesight, she would swear that the young man she had been led to believe had lain at death's door all this week had never looked fitter! And as shock filled her, all she was able to utter was the one word—his name.

Cristo!' she gasped.

CHAPTER SEVEN

STILL not over the shock of what her vision was telling her, Laine shot a look to Zare. His face, she saw, was showing not a glimmer of welcome for Cristo, nor, as he flicked a tight-lipped glance at her, was there a trace of the lover he had been only a short while ago in his look.

But Cristo was getting over his astonishment, and his exclamation of 'Laine!' was bringing her attention back to him, as he bounded forward, and without more ado gave both her cheeks a resounding kiss, then hauled her delightedly into his arms to give her a huge hug.

With Cristo's bent head somewhere beside her own, Laine was afforded a full view of Zare. She saw, his look violent, the way he checked a move that seemed as though he would tear the two of them apart. But the spurt of adrenalin that flooded her heart at the ridiculous and sudden notion that he was jealous flickered and died into nothing. For while with all her heart she would like to believe that his look of violence stemmed from nothing more than jealousy that she had so soon transferred from his arms to the arms of his brother, she knew that jealousy had nothing to do with it.

But there was no time then to decipher what thoughts were going through Zare's head; her own powers of thought had been made a nonsense before Cristo appearing out of the blue looking a superb specimen of health had brought her fresh confusion; for Cristo was looking into her face.

'What . . .!' His unbelieving exclamation did not get finished, as, with an arm still about her, he turned so that they were both facing Zare.

But suddenly, comprehension dawned on Cristo, and his grin was wide that he seemed to think he had the answer to everything—and that included the reason why his brother was favouring him with such a hostile look.

'You wanted to surprise me, didn't you, Zare?' he said, not a bit abashed that his brother's expression had not lightened at all. 'Were you going to bring Laine to see me or,' his grin was there again, 'did you calculate that I would find a month away from home too long?' And, too excited by arriving home and finding Laine there to wait for an answer, his grin looking as though it would never depart, he turned to tell her, 'And what a beautiful surprise you are. Like me, you must have just arrived too, or Zare would have been on the phone to tell me not to make any arrangements for tomorrow, when he intended bringing you to see me.'

None of it made any sense to Laine's utterly confused thoughts. Even though her eyes were telling her that Cristo was in top form, she somehow needed to establish the basic fact that her eyes were not deceiving her about the way, by the look of it, she had been deceived ever since she had got there.

'You—you are—well, Cristo?' she found her husky voice to ask.

'Never better,' he said cheerfully. Though his grin faded as he owned, lest she should think she had made the flight to Italy unnecessarily, 'But I was feeling very depressed after my illness.' And, his irrepressible grin of good humour refusing to be defeated, it was there again as he added, 'But I'm not depressed any longer.'

'Your—illness—lasted a long time,' Laine murmured, still endeavouring to pin some basic facts down.

'My body is normally healthy,' he replied. 'It didn't take me long to shake off the physical effects of being laid low.' He looked at Zare to include him in the conversation. Zare, she noted, had not said another word after that spurt of Italian that had left him when Cristo had walked in. 'I'm still ready to start work any time you say, Zare,' he said, and looking back to Laine, cheerfully he told her, 'I wanted to start work again last Monday, only late on Sunday night I got a call from my brother—from England——' he remembered, 'telling me that he could not agree with my doctors that I was as well as they said, and that I was to take myself off to the Alps for a month.'

And to the Alps, whichever Alps they were, went Laine's mind as she tried to fight her way through the fog, was where Cristo thought, had he not arrived home unexpectedly, Zare would be taking her tomorrow.

She looked at Zare again and saw he didn't look any happier that Cristo still had his arm around her. She knew then that there was only one place she was going, and that was back to England—with all speed. And . . .

'But what am I thinking of!' Cristo broke into her thoughts. 'You shouldn't be here.' He wasn't telling her anything she didn't know. 'You should be in New Zealand with your parents!'

Surfacing from her thoughts, Laine saw that whatever it was she was going to be able to sort out from the muddle up there in her head, one thing stood out very clearly—Cristo had nothing at all to do with this web of deceit that surrounded her.

'By now they should be in Australia,' she replied,

opening up to him when there was so much in her that had to be kept secret. Heavens, she couldn't escape the thought, Zare Forturini would never stop laughing if he had gleaned from her response to him that she was in love with him!

'Australia!' Cristo exclaimed. And, light breaking, 'You mean they're going to Tony's wedding after all!'

She murmured a quiet, 'Yes,' not missing the fact that Zare was looking daggers at being excluded from this private tête-à-tête.

'Oh, *cara*,' said Cristo softly, and when she hadn't a clue what his soft gentle endearment was supposed to mean, he did no more than pull her close into his arms again. 'You were looking forward to going with them so much, yet you forfeited your savings so that your dear *madre* and *padre* could see Tony mar . . .'

Zare cutting in, his voice like a thunderclap as, in English, to let her know he was as mad with her as with his brother, was abruptly ordering, 'Take your arms from the *signorina*!' Startled, Cristo dropped his arms from her as Zare, his expression as thunderous as his voice, rapped, 'Follow me to my study, I wish to talk privately to you.'

'*Mamma mia!*' broke from a startled Cristo as Zare strode out. But his good humour was never suppressed for long. 'You will excuse me, Laine, I think my brother is a little—er—cross that I have gone against his wishes and ruined your surprise visit to me tomorrow—he never was one to endure having his plans thwarted.' Though before he followed as Zare had commanded, he stayed long enough to instruct, 'You will wait here for me?'

'It's late,' Laine managed to smile, her need to get her confused thoughts into some sort of order growing desperate. 'Shall we leave it until the morning?'

Her thoughts had been charging one after the other before she had got to her room. But once there, they fairly galloped along. They chased her as she sluiced her face and prepared for bed, positively flew as she took the plate Zare had given her from her bag and propped it up on the dressing table. But by the time she had been in bed for ten minutes, her thoughts were an absolute torrent. And another ten minutes later, it was touch and go that she did not storm from her bed and break that plate she loved so much into a hundred and one pieces. She didn't of course—she still loved Zare Forturini.

My God!, she was thinking another half hour later, everything now sorted in her mind. 'Unlike you,' she could vividly recall him saying, 'I have never been ashamed of the truth.' The wretched, despicable swine, she fumed, loving him having nothing to do with her fund of low names for him, he with his abhorrence of lies! Had he had a field day!

He knew better than anyone that Cristo had fully recovered, that Cristo had been looking forward to going back to work on that Sunday that seemed light years away when he had called to tell her that Cristo's recovery was being retarded because he was pining for a sight of her. He had been lying in his teeth ever since then!

Oh, she now knew what it was all about, of course. A dab hand when it came to mixing in with his brother's love life, she no longer needed to recall his thunderous 'Take your arms from the *signorina*!' to know that there was no place for her in his plans for Cristo.

Oriana hadn't been good enough for him either. But when there had been nothing like that between her and Cristo, Zare Forturini had decided to investigate the girl he thought, from the money Cristo had told him he wanted for her, was the new girl in his young brother's life. And, since Cristo's fortune was at stake, there was only one way to discover what sort of a girl Cristo had got himself entangled with this time.

The only reason she had been lied to, conned into leaving England, was not that Cristo was ill, but that, believing that soon Cristo would say that he wanted to marry her, and with her, unlike Oriana not living in Italy, Zare Forturini, a busy man, had wanted her not in England, but under his nose where, as from Oriana's visits to the house, he could judge if Laine Balfour would make a suitable wife for Cristo.

Well, she had failed the test miserably, she thought, and was back to hating Zare again when she thought of how passionately they had kissed. Zare's kisses, those kisses that had so thrilled her, those kisses that had had her so mindless they had even had her telling him that she wanted him—oh God, she groaned as tears came to her eyes, all those kisses had been to him were just a final test to see, when her passion was aroused, just how faithful she could be to the man he thought she had her sights set on marrying.

Wiping away useless tears, Laine lay down and tried to find rest, a dozen memories of how gullible she had been coming to bombard her. Memories of how from the very first she had been so taken in that she had thought Zare's question to Anna-Maria about Cristo that Monday night they had arrived had been to ask how Cristo was. More likely, she realised, recalling the way Zare had not rushed to get them there, he had been asking if Cristo had gone yet!

Laine finally drifted off to sleep adding a few uncomplimentary names for herself, for the idiot she had been. Of course Anna-Maria was always singing—

why wouldn't she? Her prayers had been answered for the recovery of the young man she doted on—there was nothing at all the matter with him.

The first thing that met Laine's eyes when she awoke the next morning was the dear little porcelain plate she had popped up on her dressing table the night before. She got out of bed, turning her back on her sunshine plate as tears threatened. She was not going to cry, she determined, at least, not until she was safely back in England.

And England, she thought, was where she would be before she was very much older. She was determined that neither Zare Forturini nor his brother should know what an effort it cost to be down for breakfast at the usual time, but she left her room feeling broken up inside.

To find Zare alone in the breakfast room, no sign of Cristo when she had been hoping that his presence would make things easier for her, was a blow she could do nothing other than take on the chin.

'Good morning,' she greeted Zare politely, though that politeness was far more than he deserved even if he had retained the same sufficient supply of manners to get to his feet as she entered. 'Cristo not up yet?' she enquired, not giving way to the sudden urge to throw something sharp and pointed at his sardonic front.

'Unfortunately,' he replied smoothly, 'you will have to wait to see my brother. I found it necessary to send him on an errand. I fear it may take most of the day.'

The temper which up in her room she had sworn not to lose, frayed drastically at his letting her know that to keep Cristo out of her clutches, the lordly swine had invented an errand for him. But she was saved from breaking her oath, in that just then

Angelina came in with a fresh pot of coffee, and her usual toast.

Counting a further ten as she availed herself of the coffee-pot, Laine saw no reason to look at the man she hated with all her being, and loved with the whole of her heart.

'It's a pity about that,' she remarked, slowly stirring her coffee. 'I should like to have seen him again before I leave.'

'Do I take it from that that you are not staying to spend some time with him?'

'Do you think he's now fit enough—for such—antics?' she asked, her temper looking for an outlet despite any talking to it was getting from her.

'From what I saw of the pair of you last night, I thought a bucket of water would be needed to separate you,' came the snarling answer, his temper, she gathered, more than ready to meet her halfway.

At least, from Zare's remark she was able to glean the comfort that whatever he had seen last night, he had not seen that she was in love with him. Though if he thought a bucket of water was needed for her and Cristo, she had no idea what he thought would have been needed when she had been beneath him on that couch!

Warm colour threatening to invade her cheeks, Laine busied herself spreading butter on her toast. Then, when she thought she had control again, her voice cool again, she was able to comment:

'If Cristo wishes to see me, he knows he will be welcome at my home. That is,' she just couldn't resist, 'if he's well enough to come to England.'

'I see little point in my brother travelling to England to see you,' was shot back at her before she could take another breath, the fire in him fading, as he added smoothly, 'No point at all—since you will not be there.'

Had he wanted to shock her into looking at him, then he had succeeded. Having been sure, his investigation into her suitability completed, that before this breakfast time was over he would be saying that her flight arrangements had been made and would be telling her 'On your way' Laine jerked her head back to see he was leaning back in his chair, the mocking light in his eyes telling her that now he had delivered that little gem, the floor was all hers.

Grappling with fresh shock, she searched into every corner of her mind to discover just what he was up to now. But, unable to find so much as a clue, she decided that she just wasn't up to any more verbal fencing; her barb about Cristo's health had bounced right off Zare anyway.

'Correct me if I am wrong, *signore*,' she brought out stiffly, 'but are you telling me that it's *not* your intention that I fly home today?'

'Not today, tomorrow, or any other day,' he told her, and even had the nerve to look her in the eye as he added, 'until I am ready.' Though a slight softening had come to his hard attitude, she thought, although he turned the knife as he tacked on, 'And if my hearing is as good as I believe it is, you parted with any money you could have cabled for when you gave your last copper to your parents.'

Wary of him now, and right to be wary, she knew, Laine cancelled the idea that there had been any softening in him. 'But why?' she asked. 'You can't possibly want me here,' she said angrily. And as a thought struck, 'Not unless . . .'

'Unless what?' was barked at her before she could get it all of a piece in her mind.

'Unless,' she said, puzzling it out as she went, 'Unless you think . . .' her eyes shot to his, no belief in what she was saying even as she said it, 'Unless you think I would make a suitable wife for Cristo aft . . .'

'That is the *last* thing I think!' came slamming at her, mighty aggression storming on the rampage. With some difficulty, he harnessed it. But it was after several moments of silence that he very nearly sank her as he tossed over the table, 'You think I would allow you to marry my brother after the way you behaved with me last night?'

Wilting that he should not shrink from bringing that up when, from her memory of it, he had been as much involved as she, Laine came out with the only defence she could find—false as it was.

'I must be better at it than I thought, Zare,' she told him loftily, the best she could do in a pitying smile breaking from her. 'I thought with your—expertise— you would have guessed that I was just stringing you along when I told you I wanted you.'

It was that pitying look that did it, she guessed. Zare getting to his feet and moving to her side of the table told her she would have been far better off not challenging him—on this issue of all issues.

'Stringing me along, were you?' he asked, angry eyes going down to her mouth as he rasped, 'We'll prove that, shall we?'

At once Laine was ready to back off. But it was too late for that. Firm hands were on her arms as he lifted her out of her chair, and before she knew it she was in his arms with his mouth coming down to assault hers. And struggle though she might, he would not let her go.

And soon, as she had been afraid would happen, he had her treacherous body reacting to him. For even as she sought to hate him, she was finding her love was the stronger of those two strongest of all emotions.

Unable to best the mammoth pull he had for her, her senses swam, entirely unaware, as their bodies pressed closer, yet even closer together, when it was that the hands and arms that had pushed at him were suddenly around him, or that she was clinging on to him as if her life depended upon it.

And then all at once she was free, and having to come back to the bewilderment of reality. For Zare had pushed her away, angry with her and with himself, for he, she knew from that close contact with him, had not been unaffected either.

Though he was the one to surface first. He the one to remember the reason for him taking her in his arms in the first place. But as he slammed from the room, the crash of the door behind him told her he was too furious to bother who heard, then his cutting parting remark of, 'Shamming *that*, were you!' made Laine absolutely livid.

Fuming at how easily he had got to her, she was already storming up to her room when she heard his car roar down the drive. By the sound of it, for he never drove his car like that, Zare too was still as mad as hell.

Eventually her impotent fury waned, and it was then that Laine put her mind to seek the answer to the two questions that sought priority. The first, how on earth was she to get back to England? The second, why in the name of creation was Zare so determined that she should not leave?

By the time evening arrived, having had all day in which to puzzle it out, for neither Zare nor Cristo had returned for lunch, she thought that perhaps she had the answer to the second and, she hoped, the first.

The only possible answer to why Zare was making her stay 'until I am ready' just had to be that, having all the evidence he needed that she would *not* make a suitable wife for his brother, Zare, believing that Cristo was in love with her, was making her stay so that Cristo should eventually see her in her true colours.

Sure that must be the answer, Laine was still trying to fill in the large hole that appeared in her reasoning. Why, when she would have thought Zare would be throwing them together the sooner to have the scales fall from his brother's eyes, had he, at the crack of dawn by the look of it, sent Cristo off on an errand that meant they had seen nothing at all of each other for the whole of the day?

But it was just then that she heard the sound of a car. And, anxious that should it be Cristo returning that she had the answer to the question which had now become urgent, that question—how was she to get back to England—she waited only to hear that the masculine footsteps that passed her door were different from the sound of Zare's firm tread, then as a door along the landing opened and then closed, she slipped from her room.

Nerves attacked her at the risk she was taking, for she was in no hurry after this morning to see Zare again. Laine listened at several of the doors until she thought she heard a sound coming from within one of the rooms.

Hoping with all her heart that it would not be Zare who answered her knock, quickly, while she still had some courage, she lifted her hand to the woodwork, knocked, and waited.

'Laine!' exclaimed Cristo, and she was relieved to see, since half the buttons on his shirt were undone, that it was him. 'Come in for a minute,' he invited, obviously pleased to see her. 'I was just going to take a shower, but that can wait a while.'

What she wanted to ask him was private. Laine needed no second bidding as she took him up on his invitation. She did not want to wait until after dinner when, depending what was in his head, Zare might or might not leave them alone together.

'You've been out on an errand, I hear,' she said, as it occurred to her that since he was going to think it odd anyway that she wanted to leave straightaway when as far as he knew she had only just got there, then it might be better if she led up to ask what she had to ask him.

'Wouldn't you know it,' he said with a smile, inviting her to take a bedroom chair while he lounged against the end of his bed. 'Zare heard late last night that there were some papers which an uncle of ours in Florence wanted to look through before a business meeting tomorrow.'

'You've been to Florence?' she asked, thinking what she had to ask could be said better standing up as she declined the chair and wished he had taken her to Florence with him, given her the money she was going to ask for the loan of, and left her there.

Cristo nodded. 'And once there, neither my aunt nor uncle would hear of anything but that I stayed to lunch.' His grin was there again as he said, 'They would have had me staying to dinner too if they could, only I wanted to get back to you. I thought you and I might go out for the evening—there is so much of my country I should like to show you.'

'That would be lovely,' Laine agreed, delaying in what she wanted to ask him as it came to her to wonder, with Cristo wanting to take a shower, if perhaps later, while they were out, might not be a better time to bring up the subject of her wanting him to loan her her air fare.

But before she could come to any conclusion, he was asking if she had heard from her parents since they had been away. And when she replied that she had, he was asking how they were liking New Zealand, and before she could answer:

'But of course,' he was remembering, 'they must be either in, or on their way to Australia by now,' a gentle look coming her way, warming her because she hadn't had to tell him why she was not with them, he had guessed, from what he knew of her, the reason she had stayed behind. 'It's this Saturday that Tony gets married, if I remember the date correctly.'

'That's right,' Laine agreed, the memory of her happy family stirring a need in her to be with them, to be there to see Tony married herself. Unbeknown to her, her eyes had clouded over, and brought forth the sympathetic comment:

'It's a pity you cannot be there too, isn't it?' Then astonished her as he remarked, 'I should hate it if I had to forgo seeing my brother's wedding.'

'Zare's not getting married, is he!' The exclamation had left her before she could hold it back. Even as she knew that she stood not the smallest chance of marrying Zare herself, she just could not bear to think of him marrying anyone else.

'You sound as surprised as I would be if that were the case,' said Cristo with his familiar grin. 'Though there have been one or two who thought they were in there with a chance.' He paused, then said quietly, 'Oriana, for one.'

'Oriana? But I thought—thought she was your girl-friend?'

'She latched on to me when she saw she was getting nowhere with Zare,' he revealed, causing her to look at him in some surprise, especially at his words 'latched on'.

'But you were—in love with her,' she protested, despite the evidence that he could be no longer in love, by the way he was speaking of Oriana.

'I was infatuated with her,' he corrected with a smile. 'Although,' he owned, 'it did not feel like mere infatuation at the time—nor was I able to see then that Zare only ever does things for my own good.'

'You were very down when you first came to England,' Laine inserted quickly, not wanting to be reminded that it was for Cristo's own good that she was being made to stay.

'I was lovesick for Oriana, and not seeing at all what a terrific brother I have in Zare,' he replied, and positively beamed at her as he added, 'Look at Zare getting you here, for a start,' before he returned to the subject of Oriana. 'He saw before I did that she was only after my family's money—six months after he had sent me away, she married a man who has little to recommend him but his wallet. Zare came personally to England to break the news to me, but I was already cured of my infatuation.'

'So the news he brought you—didn't hurt?'

'Not a scrap. By then I had been taken wholeheartedly as a substitute member of your family, and,' he said cheerfully, 'I was enjoying every moment of being fussed over by your mother, taken to his pub by your father, and being treated like a brother by you.'

It did Laine's heart good to hear Cristo talk of her family that way. By the sound of it, he had lapped up every minute spent with them.

'But it wasn't to last much longer, was it?' she said,

a harsh memory breaking of the way, when he had been so poorly, Zare had insisted he return to Italy. 'Was it for your own good too that he recalled you?'

'He only ordered me home because . . .' Looking at him as he broke off, she saw the dull flush of colour that came up under Cristo's skin. 'Because . . .' he tried again. But again he could not finish.

And Laine, knowing he had told Zare one very big lie, saw then that Cristo was not at all happy with lies, in that he was stuck to say something which was not the truth.

'Your brother recalled you,' she filled in for him, no longer able to smile at him, 'because you wrote and asked for an advance of money so that you could give it to me.'

'He told you about it!' Cristo broke out, looking astonished. But he succeeded in astonishing her, when, putting his own astoundment to one side, he exclaimed, 'The money wasn't for you! It was for your mother! I wanted to give her . . .'

'My *mother*!' Shock at what he was saying had her speechless for a couple of seconds. Then Laine, as proud as either of her parents, was rushing in hotly to repudiate what he had said. 'My mother would never take money from you—she wouldn't take money from any . . .'

'I know that *now*,' he came in quickly to cool her heat. 'But at the time I was hopeful that she would.' He paused, his look apologetic. 'Forgive me, Laine,' he continued, 'but I could see how things were— financially—with your family. Just as I could see that it was breaking your father's heart that with Australia only next door to New Zealand, he could just not afford to see his beloved son married. To be so near and yet so far was a terrible blow to him, I could see that when he read Tony's letter. It was then,' he expanded, 'when I could have got sufficient money to pay for the whole trip for the three of you, that seeing how proud you all were, I decided that two thousand pounds would perhaps be large enough without being so large as to cause offence.'

'You offered money to my *father*!' Laine exclaimed, not at all surprised in the circumstances that she was getting it all wrong, when Cristo shook his head.

'I knew your father was not the one to approach,' he put her right, having seen for himself, she saw, that her father would have had a fit if he had. 'But I was hopeful that your mother would accept my gift and perhaps find a right moment to tell your father about it—it was such a small sum, after all,' he ended, causing her to blink.

But in coming to terms with the fact that two thousand pounds was neither here nor there to the Forturinis, Laine did not want to leave it there.

'So you wrote to your brother and told him you wanted the money for me?' she questioned—and saw that Cristo was still looking a shade uncomfortable when, after a moment or two, he said:

'I didn't write that I wanted the money for Laine— but Elaine,' and he paused again, then was saying, 'Perhaps I'd better explain,' breaking off again before, as though searching for the most tactful way of explaining anything, he went on, 'My brother can be very—tough—when it comes to looking after my interests. I had good reason to know that when . . .'

'When he sent you to England to break your friendship with Oriana?' Laine prompted to help him out.

'Exactly,' he said, confessing, 'I think I must have been in a very sensitive state at that particular time, for when, not caring if I were king or pauper, you and your family made me so welcome and warmed my bruised heart, I was afraid that if I so much as mentioned any of you to Zare he would be on the next plane to England to—to . . .'

'To see if we too, like Oriana, were after your money?'

'Ridiculous, wasn't I?' said Cristo. 'Had Zare come over and met you all, he would have seen at once that he need not trouble himself in his safeguarding of my interests. He has seen that now, of course,' he inserted, 'or he would not have brought you here. But, as I have said, I was in a sensitive state at the time, so I said not one word to him about my new friends. And later,' he went on, still struggling to find the right tactful words, she guessed, as with many pauses, he told her, 'when I wanted the advance, I became conscious of the odd scrape here and there I have in the past got myself into, which Zare has had to extract me from—conscious of the worry I have been to him. Perhaps being away from Italy has made me more responsible that it was about time I ceased giving him cause to worry about me—anyway,' he ploughed on, 'I had cause to know when he saw, where I had not, that Oriana had greedy fingers, that he thought I still had a lot to learn about women.'

'But why,' inserted Laine, not able to see the sense of it at all, 'write and tell him that you wanted the money for me? I know at the time you still thought I was going to travel with my parents, but . . .'

'I wasn't thinking of you when I wrote Elaine, but your mother,' he corrected her.

'My . . .' Laine broke off, getting more confused the more tactful he was trying to be. 'But,' she was then pointing out, 'while I grant you that my mother's name is Elaine too, I only ever heard you call her Ella!'

Perhaps Cristo saw her confusion, for it was with his look apologetic still that, after taking a deep breath, he plunged to let some light in.

'With my never having breathed a word about any of you, it came to me, since Zare was going to want to know why I wanted an advance, and since I could not possibly lie to him, that if I wrote and said I wanted the money to give as a present to my friend Mrs Balfour, then straightaway he would think I had got myself involved with a married lady.'

'But why not say Ella?' Laine questioned, the mist starting to clear.

'It is a pet name, I think,' said Cristo, obviously never having come across any other English female bearing that name as a full christian name. 'With Zare thinking I knew little about women, my thoughts were that equally he would think I was very involved with the lady, that I can call her by a pet name.'

To Laine's way of thinking, Zare could be forgiven for thinking that his brother must be deeply involved with any woman who would take two thousand pounds from him.

'So you see,' said Cristo, looking ready to breathe a sigh of relief that all that was out of the way, 'why it was that I wrote to him and said I wished to make a gift to my friend Elaine.'

Laine thought that she did see—just as she saw that with Zare thinking that the money had been promised, he had advanced it rather than have Cristo break his word. It was by way of putting a full stop to all that had been said then that she told Cristo:

'But you could have saved yourself all that trouble. My mother didn't take your gift.'

'Your mother is a very gracious lady,' said Cristo, his grin surfacing after being in hiding for so long. 'I was so afraid, when she pushed the money back at me as though burned, that I had offended her unforgivably. But a moment later she laughed, the way she does,' he remembered affectionately, 'and made me feel immediately better, although I was running a fever at the time, by saying, just as if I was Tony, "I just don't know what I'm going to do with you, young man!"'

A smile broke from Laine, the scene so vivid in her mind she could almost hear her mother saying it. But Cristo's voice was breaking in, his voice warm with the affection he had for them all, as he said quietly:

'I have never known such a proud family.'

To her way of thinking, remembering Zare and his autocratic arrogance, the Forturini family were right up there with them. But the Balfour pride in her was to dip when, without thinking about it, the words fell from her:

'Cristo, as a friend of my proud family, would you think me very dreadful if—without pride—I asked you to lend me my air fare back to England?'

His surprise covered any awkwardness she might have felt at her question. 'You want to return to England!' he exclaimed. 'But—but you've only just got here!'

Searching desperately hard to find an excuse that would keep him in ignorance of not only all that had gone on between her and Zare, but more importantly, something that would keep him from knowing that, idiotically, she had fallen head over heels in love with his brother, pink coloured her cheeks at the thought that, when he had been so open with her, she was going to have to lie to Cristo.

She half turned from him, knowing that he would be less likely to believe her lies if he saw her pink colour.

But he had seen her colour, and had taken it for for the colour of embarrassment that she had had to sink her pride, she was to hear. For he had swiftly left his position by the bed end, and had come over to her.

'Forgive me, Laine,' he apologised, at once. 'Do not be embarrassed, little English sister, that you have had to ask,' he said, trying to help her over that embarrassment. 'Of course I will pay your air ticket,' he told her stoutly.

She suddenly wanted to weep at his kindness. She felt sad that when what she had wanted was promised, she just did not want to go, but wanted to stay—with Zare. When Cristo's arm came about her and he looked into her eyes, she was unable to prevent that sadness from showing.

'You are unhappy?' he asked, his face serious as he urged, 'Can you not tell me the reason why you want to leave us? Some—Englishman, perhaps?'

Dumbly Laine shook her head lest the words came blurting from her that it was not that she *wanted* to leave, but that she *had* to leave. And she was grateful that Cristo, as sensitive as he had shown himself to be, questioned her no further, but said:

'By the look of your sad eyes, you wish to be away with all haste,' and his other arm coming around her, he said quietly, 'Leave it to me, *cara*. I will arrange it.'

And gently then, when, still mute, she offered him the best she could in the way of a smile, he bent his head to seal his promise to help, with what would have been a light kiss to her mouth.

Only before their lips could meet, a hair's breadth separating their two mouths, such a bellow of outrage was heard from the door that, like two people caught in some clandestine meeting, they sprang apart, Cristo's arms shooting from around her, as guiltily they both looked to see an enraged Zare standing by the door.

Never had Laine, who had seen him angry before, ever seen him look as furious as he was then. The blaze from his eyes threatened murder as his fierce glare went to where Cristo, his shirt unbuttoned, had been delayed taking his shower in his pleasure at finding Laine at his door.

Cristo's fingers going to button up his shirt as he realised how things must look had not helped to cool the volcanic fury that was burning up in Zare, Laine saw. And she knew then, as he pushed the door wide, that at any moment now there were going to be ructions that he had come home to find Laine Balfour being entertained in his brother's bedroom!

CHAPTER EIGHT

Rooted by the barely concealed violence she saw in Zare, certain from the way his hands were clenched at his sides that any moment now would see him setting about the pair of them, Laine saw the giant effort he made to control the need she saw in him to physically flatten the pair of them.

Like her, Cristo had been struck dumb by the towering rage his brother was in, and the silence that had followed that roar of outrage at the compromising situation he had come across was broken by Zare. His tone taut with the restraint he was exercising, it was to her that he addressed his first remarks:

'You will be good enough, *signorina*,' he clipped, his voice arctic, 'to leave my brother's bedroom.' Not expecting any refusal, he stood away from the door, not finished yet as Laine, her head tilted proudly, angry that he was daring to think what he was thinking, moved forward. 'You will oblige me,' he carried on as she drew level with him, 'by remembering that while you are a guest in my house, as far as you are concerned, this particular room is out of bounds.'

Wanting to do some physical setting about herself at that remark, the appalled gasp of, '*Zare!*' that came from Cristo as the ice cold insolence in his brother's remark brought him from his stricken silence gave Laine some of the control she had seen Zare use. Though how she quelled the almost unsurmountable urge to let fly with her hand as, unspeaking, she passed through the doorway, she did not know.

A volley of Italian had broken out behind her before she had reached her room, Zare's voice, still ice-cold, axeing through anything heated that came from Cristo. But by then her own fury had peaked. The humiliating memory of being ordered from Cristo's room, just as though she were some—some tart!—made her bitterly regret that she had not taken a swipe at Zare as all her senses had demanded.

Her pride was still sorely aggrieved when, not many minutes later, she heard a door along the landing crash to like the sound of thunder, followed by the sound of footsteps drawing near as the thunder rolled away. If she wasn't mistaken, Cristo had been sorted out—now it was her turn!

But she did not need to see the dark expression on Zare's face to know that he was still being ridden hard by fury. The fact that he had barged his way into her room without the politeness of knocking told her that he was too angry to let his inborn good manners surface. That, or that he was of the opinion that her behaviour had forfeited her the right to even the smallest courtesy.

That thought alone did nothing to cool the proud indignation with which Laine was awash with. 'To what do I owe the honour of your visit?' she let fly first, the narrowing of his eyes telling her that her sarcastic tongue was doing her no favours.

'It occurred to me,' he replied curtly, 'that one of us should inform you that your affair with my brother is at an end.'

'My . . .' was as far as she got.

'So too,' he chopped her off, when she had just about grown sick and tired of his high-handed way of not wanting to hear her out, 'are any hopes you had of marrying him!'

High-handed just wasn't the word for the way he was being with her, Laine thought. In her view she had suffered enough humiliation at his hands for one day. She wasn't interested in marrying Cristo, but it wasn't up to his brother to decide that issue for her.

'Forgive me, *signore*,' she said tightly, 'but I was not aware that I had to have your permission before I decided whom I should or should not marry.'

His jaw clenched, but she had pride as her ally when weakness would have invaded that he was growing more incensed, not because she was not denying that she had her sights set on marrying his brother, but that she was daring to stand up to him.

But he still had that iron-hard control about him, she saw, when, turning for the door as though as far as he was concerned, having told her bluntly what he had come to tell her, the interview was over, he let fall:

'I agree, *signorina*, you do not need my permission. But, if Cristoforo marries before he is thirty-five, then to do so without my consent will lose him his inheritance.'

He would have left her room then without another word. But resentment was riding high in Laine that not only had he not bothered to look at her while delivering his parting shot, but that he should dare to wear that arrogant look that said he thought her beneath him.

'And you don't think I'm good enough to be your sister-in-law, is that it?' she fired indignantly before he could have the door open, her feet taking her right up to him, her chin thrust at an aggressive angle as she waited for him to reply to her outraged challenge.

For long seconds he studied her. Then, ignoring the sparks that were shooting from her anger-darkened eyes, he told her loftily:

'We both know you possess a surfeit of passion, *signorina*. You think I should accept you for a sister when I have knowledge of how that passion has you forgetting every other man when I arouse it?' And if being so insolently reminded of how much she had wanted him, wasn't enough to make her want to hit him, when he reached for the doorknob and said, 'Cristoforo is leaving for Milan very shortly, but should that excess of passion become too much for you to cope with,' pausing to look mockingly at her before he continued, 'then if you come to me, I will see what I can do for you,' Laine's temper went wild.

But her hand didn't have time to start stinging from the cutting blow it had flown through the air to serve him before, in an instant, his cool manner gone, Zare had gripped hold of her upper arms in a brutal hold.

Unrepentant, even if fear did strike her at the terrible uncontrolled wrath in those dark eyes that scorched into hers, Laine's heart was stampeding, because it looked very much as though she was either going to feel her own face stinging—or be brutally kissed.

But, when ageless seconds passed while he fought for control, suddenly she was free. Suddenly Zare had thrust her away. And abruptly it was that he pulled open the door, his voice grim, as he pronounced:

'I will see you at dinner.'

'Not tonight you won't,' she shouted after him. 'I'd rather starve than eat at your table!' she yelled the moment before she threw the door shut behind him. Two seconds later, she broke down in a flood of tears.

Half an hour after that, with no clear memory of what thoughts had gone through her mind save that she still loved the lordly arrogant swine, Laine went to rinse her face.

But it was as she came from her bathroom, determined not to cry any more, that the sound of a car starting up had her going to her bedroom window to watch and to see that it was Cristo at the wheel as a car swung round from the rear of the house.

'Oh no!' The words broke from her even as the car picked up velocity and went speeding down the hill.

The tyrant, the viper! she becalled Zare as catastrophe struck. She had been too upset to recall him saying, 'Cristoforo is leaving for Milan very shortly,' too upset to wonder until now what Cristo going to Milan would do to her plans. But that monster had sent him away and—oh, how was she going to get back to England now!

She was no further forward with finding an answer when, either taking her at her word that she would not be joining him for dinner, or having had enough of her that day too, a light tap on her door showed that Zare had sent Angelina to bring her dinner to her room.

Though Laine had partaken of some of the coffee that had accompanied her meal, tears threatening all the time, she had been too upset to eat. But when she opened her eyes the following morning, remembering with clarity all that had happened since Zare had returned home last evening; when her eyes went to the table where she was expecting to see the meal tray just where she had left it, a small cry of surprise left her.

But her surprise was not on seeing that the tray was no longer there, but from seeing that whoever had tiptoed in to remove it while she had been asleep had left in its place what appeared to be a bulging envelope. Curiosity astir, she threw back the covers and went to investigate.

A short while later, a heap of money on the table in front of her, Laine had the knowledge that Cristo had kept his word. The money he had enclosed with his letter was for her train fare and any expenses she might incur—for her flight, he had written, was booked to England. All that she had to do was to get from Valgaro to the airport in Bologna by Tuesday afternoon.

Pushing aside what she saw looked to be ample funds to get her to the airport by tomorrow afternoon, Laine again took up the letter and read through once more all that Cristo had written. She noted from the extensive list of train times that he had even included quite a few other getting-on and getting-off railway stations in case, with her lack of Italian, she found herself on a train which she should not be on. He seemed to know she would not be asking Zare to give her a lift anywhere.

Dear sweet Cristo! she thought, getting misty-eyed again. Even if he did not understand what was going on, he had not let her down. She guessed then that he must have given the envelope to Anna-Maria to pass to her when she had an opportunity. For had the envelope been entrusted to Angelina, she would have received it last night when Angelina had brought her her meal.

Turning her back on that part of her that was foolish enough never to want to leave, Laine re-read all that Cristo had written.

'Dear Laine,' he had begun, 'You will have gathered by now that when my brother gets angry—*he gets angry*! Though never have I before known him in the kind of rage he was in tonight—such a rage that it was impossible to talk to him. However, by the time you receive this letter I am sure he will have recovered his temper, and will have apologised to you for the wrong thoughts that made him so angry when he saw you in my arms in my bedroom.'

Put like that, it did sound bad, Laine had to admit, but she read on:

'With Zare refusing to let me get a word in to tell him that I look upon you as the very dear sister I never had, the outcome of his fury is that, since I appear to have energy to spare, there is work to be done in one of our Milan offices. So, Laine, I am banished. But we will see each other again, be assured of that. For I have no intention of losing touch with my English family, and none at all of not seeing again my English sister who, in my delirium when I was ill, I believed was the only one who—like you did before—could fetch for me some soothing cough syrup.'

Moist-eyed, Laine read the details that followed about her flight and the many train times and what to do if she went wrong somewhere. Then Cristo was signing off, 'I wish you a good flight—maybe one day you will be able to tell your Italian brother why it is that you must return to England in such a hurry.'

Laine popped the letter together with the money he had given her into her bag, and went to get showered and dressed with her mind only half on the packing she had to do, as she tried to deny herself the need to see Zare just once more before she left.

That once he had left for his work would see her leaving soon afterwards, made her give in to the compulsion to go downstairs and join him for breakfast. For if she was to get to Bologna by tomorrow, as she saw it, she had better leave Valgaro today.

That compulsion to see Zare made her put aside any thoughts on how she was going to feel if he was still in the same foul temper he had been in last night. She just had to see him once more before she left.

To find when she had the courage to walk into the breakfast room, that Zare was where he was at this time every morning, his former good manners returned as he rose and waited for her to be seated before again taking his seat, sent her heart pounding away agonisingly within her. She didn't know then how she could go, but knew that go she had to.

'You are—well, this morning?' he asked formally, his manner stiff, though the fury that had been in him the evening before gone.

'Quite well, thank you,' she replied. Angelina coming in with her breakfast gave her a moment in which to see that, though she hardly thought that Zare was regretting his rage of last night, this morning he was bent on playing the perfect host. Very well, she thought, and taking his lead, she prepared to be the perfect guest.

Though only five minutes later she was beginning to feel a little niggled. Never had Zare been *this* polite to her! It was all very well knowing that the last thing she wanted was a row with him, now of all times. But, answering a well-brought-up, 'Yes, thank you,' to his—was her breakfast satisfactory, a prim, 'No, thank you,' to his—is there anything else you require? she felt as though she was breakfasting with a perfect stranger. And she did not like it.

Irritation warred with sadness in her. Tears were close that this was goodbye, but crossness that she had come down to breakfast at all kept those tears at bay—this man opposite was a stranger, not the Zare Forturini she knew.

Ready to return to her room, she made a small movement to get to her feet. But that movement was halted when suddenly, as if against his will, his voice stiff, formal still, Zare said:

'It has occurred to me that—time might not lie so heavily with you, if I arranged an outing for you.'

A spurt of anger nullified her weakness of wanting to cry. By the look of it, for all he had bluntly told her that she had no chance of marrying Cristo, he was still intent on keeping her there.

'An outing, *signore*?' she replied, trying to hold down on her anger that the perfect host was seeing it as his duty that she should not be bored. 'Might I ask where you have in mind?—The hospital, perhaps?' she tossed at him sarcastically.

Oh, my word! she thought, as she saw the flicker of matching ire that crossed his features at her sarcasm. But, not sure if she was glad or sorry, she saw too the way he controlled it, his voice even, as he replied:

'There is a town not too far away which is preserved as a national monument. I thought, since you so appreciated the beauty of Siena, that a visit to San Gimignano might be of interest to you.'

Oh, Zare, she thought, wanting nothing better than to see this national monument, her anger a small thing, she was discovering. But as weak tears again threatened, she needed that anger back. But it was her attempt to find an ally in sarcasm that had her tongue unwary, as she answered snappily:

'The only outing I'm interested in is one back to England!'

Damning her tongue, more than aware how easily he could put two and two together, for one heart-stopping moment she wondered if she had given too much away.

'Tough on you,' came back the sharp answer, his tone very different from the way it had been. And, relieved that he could not have seen that her plans to return to England were already laid, instead of charging full pelt into the fray as in the past she had not hesitated to do, she just could not hold back a small smile.

Zare's eyes on her mouth, that narrowing of his eyes, had her panicky again for a few seconds as her smile departed. He never missed a thing, did Zare—was it suspicion she read in that narrow-eyed look?

Relief came again when, thinking she had better make tracks for her room before she made any more slips of the tongue to give him something to be really suspicious over, she stood up. Zare rose too, his expression bland, not so much as a glimmer of suspicion about him that she could see.

He walked with her to the door. And dearly did Laine want one last look at him, for soon she would hear his car going down the drive.

Holding hard on the impulse to look at him, as he went with her into the hall, Laine did her best to behave as if this was just an everyday parting. But she had gone towards the stairs, leaving him to go which way he would, when having thought he had accepted that she did not want to be dropped off at San Gimignano when he went out, her knees almost buckled to hear him call after her:

'If you do change your mind about wanting an outing, *signorina*, I shall be in my study.'

Gripping hard on to the banister rail, Laine turned slowly. 'You're not—going to work today!' she exclaimed, hoping with all she had that he would think that her surprise stemmed from nothing more than that she thought it unusual when every other day had seen him leaving the house at the same time.

For long moments he studied her waiting face.

Then there it was, that insincere smile she had no belief in. 'Even I, *signorina*,' he said softly, 'have the occasional day off.'

Why choose today of all days to have a day off! A severe blow dealt to her plans, Laine paced the floor of her room, trying to think that since she had no idea how frequently Zare had a day off, it could well be quite normal for him not to go to work on Mondays.

But he's always busy, came a counter-argument, as she remembered Cristo telling her ages ago that Zare's work was food and drink to him. Though since he had stated he would be in his study, that meant he would still be working—perhaps he had some business plan he had to work on and wanted to do it in the peace and quiet of his own home, went her thoughts, as she tried to oust the frightening thought that he had suspected she was up to something.

Why should it bother him if she was up to anything anyway? she thought crossly a few minutes later. Though remembering his 'Tough on you,' when she had said that the only outing she was interested in was one back to England, she had to discount that if she went to his study and today asked him for her air fare, his reply would be any different from the sort of reply he had given her before.

Again she wondered why it was that Zare Forturini was insisting that she stay just where she was. But, when several times she had been able to come up with an answer—once that she was there to wait until Cristo was better; another because she thought Zare wanted to see if she was a suitable wife for Cristo; and yet another, that Zare wanted her to be there so that the scales should fall from Cristo's eyes—this time she could come up with nothing. And in the end, she gave up trying. More important was that she thought of some way to get Anna-Maria to ring for a taxi for her without Zare being aware of it, and for—somehow— that taxi to arrive *and* depart, with her safely ensconced inside, without Zare Forturini knowing anything about it.

She was in the middle of wondering if by signs and gestures she could get Anna-Maria to understand that she wanted the taxi to wait for her at the bottom of the long drive, wondering if she could sneak out with her suitcase to meet it, when suddenly she heard the sound of a vehicle start up.

All her senses alert, in less than no time, her ears by now able to tell the difference between the Land Rover engine and the purr of Zare's car, she had grabbed up her bag and was making for her bedroom door. Her eyes caught sight of her dear porcelain plate, and while she had no compunction about leaving her clothes behind and there was no time to pack, her hand had snatched up the plate, and it was in her bag without her even having to think about it.

On noiseless feet she sped down the stairs, lucky to find the front door open—either Anna-Maria or Angelina gone to the kitchen for a broom or something with which to sweep the step, she guessed.

Haring outside, Laine knew yet more relief as the Land Rover trundled into view, and halted when Giuseppe saw her racing towards it.

His face was a picture of astonishment when, not wasting any time, she opened the passenger door and got in beside him. But this was one occasion when she was glad of their language barrier, because it saved her a whole lot of false explanation as, 'Siena,' she told him, and when he still looked startled, more firmly she repeated, 'Siena, Giuseppe, *per favore.*'

Relief was hers again when the Land Rover started

to roll forward once more, Giuseppe obviously
understanding that she wanted a lift with him to
Siena. Though she was still on edge until the vehicle
was clear of the drive and Giuseppe put his foot down.

She wondered if he always went as fast as the
vehicle would allow on his trips to Siena, and what his
business there was. For invariably he was always away
a good two hours. About to try and get through to him
that she wanted to be put down at the *stazione*, Laine
changed her mind. It was possible he might mention
when he got back in a couple of hours' time that he
had given her a lift—she did not want Zare to have too
much of a clue to where she had gone.

Not that Zare would care all that much she thought,
sadness touching her at the truth of that. In all
probability he would give a Latin shrug of his
shoulders, mutter the Italian equivalent of 'foiled
again' and tack on, 'Thank God'.

Giuseppe had made good time, she saw from her
watch when, interpreting her signs correctly that he
could let her off anywhere that was convenient to him,
he set her down.

'*Grazie*, Giuseppe,' she said. 'Goodbye,' she
whispered after the departing Land Rover.

She tried to shake off her sadness at having severed
her last link with that house at Valgaro, by taking out
Cristo's letter and making a mental note of the train
she would catch.

But on finding herself in the streets and alleyways of
a Siena that was never more beautiful now that she
was leaving, Laine saw that she had no particular need
to hurry. She had made it away from Valgaro, away
from Zare, and it could be another couple of hours
before anyone back there knew that she had left. And
anyway, with Zare at work in his study, there was a

good chance that no one would interrupt him to say that the Signorina Laine had decided to go into town.

Why should any of it bother her anyway—she was free now, for goodness' sake! Laine found no pleasure in the thought.

It was no consolation that she had hoodwinked Zare who didn't have the smallest notion that her flight had already been booked, or that her shoulder-bag housed the wherewithal to get her home, she walked on, knowing an overwhelming desire to be back in her room, back where Zare still thought her to be.

Perhaps I shall feel better when I'm back in England, she mused, and wondered just who she thought she was kidding. As she tried to rouse herself from her feeling of depression, her spirits were to be lifted when, through an arched passageway, she caught sight of the Piazza del Campo.

Oh, how the Campo beckoned! A quick look at her watch told her that she still had ample time. Just one last tiny look, said a voice that just refused to be quietened; and Laine's footsteps were taking her through the archway. And she was spellbound again by that scene that had been photographed in her mind, her ears picking up again that same echoing sound she had heard before.

How could she have missed seeing the Gaia Fountain? she wondered, remembering Zare telling her of the rectangular structure when he had been enthralling her with his description of the Palio.

Unconscious of time, at last Laine turned her back on the Gaia Fountain and her fascination with the smart way the pigeons quenched their thirst from the water jets. But when she knew that she should be getting on, she was caught in the spell of all around her.

So much was she caught that when the idea lit of lingering for perhaps ten minutes longer, to sit where she had sat before with a cup of coffee, she was thinking mutinously, why shouldn't she? Zare would not come looking for her, and even if he did, since good manners had decreed in the past that he didn't make a show of her in public, the last thing he would do would be to try and drag her back to his home. Besides—sadness hit her a heavy blow—she would never see Siena again.

The matter settled, soon she was sitting before an orange cloth-covered table, a cup of coffee before her as she stared at the Mangia Tower facing her. Her mood of rebellion gone, from nowhere came the startling thought, was she, in some Freudian fashion, hanging about in the hope that Zare would come after her?

That thought alone was sufficient to make her get to her feet and settle her bill. She knew it had not been what she had been hoping. How could it be? She loved Zare—he did not even *like* her.

But, on her feet, Laine saw she had better make tracks for the station. As yet she had no idea where she would lay her head that night. But once clear of Siena, should it be the halfway mark of Florence—where according to Cristo's timetable it was only an hour and a half's journey by train to Bologna—or be it a hotel in Bologna that she stayed that night, Cristo had given her more than enough to settle any hotel bill.

About to put on a burst of speed, the sooner to get to the station and take the first train she could, she found she could not resist standing for one more moment to let her eyes complete the semi-circle of the scene that had gripped her since first she had come across it.

The memory etched in her mind for ever, slowly Laine turned from her study to the other tall, less noted buildings that had been behind her.

And suddenly something was compelling her to look up. Something was forcing her to raise her eyes to the balconies above her. Unable to disobey that force outside herself, Laine looked along the iron-railed balconies, her eyes only stopping—as she thought her heart would stop—when they came into contact with the tall, dark-haired man standing on a balcony to the left of her.

Conscious of nothing but shock, her heart raced to catch up the stunned seconds of her seeing the man whose eyes had been scanning the area, but who now had his eyes on no one but her.

He seemed as frozen as she in that split second of their eyes meeting. But as Zare, the first to recover, called out, 'Laine!' Laine's limbs found the freedom to move. 'Wait!' she thought she heard him call—but she was waiting for nothing.

Panicking wildly, she had no idea where she was going when her feet took off. And there was no recollection at all in her of the thoughts she had had that even if Zare did follow her, he could not very well drag her back to that house at Valgaro. Indeed, she was in such a panic just then that all that she was thinking was that he had come for her—but that she couldn't allow that.

Darting madly through streets her feet had sauntered in earlier, Laine was too worked up to be bothered by any language barrier when she saw a taxi with its cargo disembarking. And before the last customer could close the door after him, she was into the back seat, afraid someone else might beat her to it, and telling the taxi driver, who looked to be the sort to take anything in his stride:

'*Stazione, per favore.*'

Though before they had gone more than a few hundred yards Laine, still panicking, was changing her mind about going to the railway station in Siena, and was conjuring up the name of one of the stations between Siena and Florence, the better to put Zare off the scent.

'Empoli *stazione*,' she leaned forward to tell the taxi driver, and went into near heart failure again when he took his eyes off the road to turn round and show her that he wasn't so able to take everything in his stride after all.

'Empoli?' he repeated.

'*Si*,' she said as firmly as she could. 'Empoli *stazione*.'

To Laine that taxi ride seemed to go on for ever. But by the time they reached Empoli and she had paid off the driver, she was feeling far calmer than she had been.

Though during what seemed another age-long wait before the Florence train came in, her nerves were to attack again and again. Each time she heard a fresh footfall, her eyes would dart to their owner in fear that Zare, somehow a mind-reader, had followed her.

Ridiculous was not the word for it, she thought when at last she sat aboard the Florence-bound train. She must be crazy in the first place to think that Zare would be interested in following her anywhere. Apart from the fact that he had no idea that she now had sufficient in her possession to afford her the use of the Italian railways—and if he had known, would not know that she had selected Empoli station in preference to the station in Siena—he would not be bothering to chase her.

By the time the train pulled into Florence, Laine

was seeing clearly that Zare had not called out 'Wait!' at all when he had seen her from that balcony in the Campo. His shout of 'Laine!' she saw then, had only come from his utter surprise at seeing her there at all. Quite clearly, she realised, he had discovered a need to make a trip to Siena in connection with the work he had been busy with, and still thinking her up in her room, he had been amazed to see her there. His shout of her name simply bore out that amazement.

On the unhappy returning thought that he would be saying 'Thank God!' to have got her out of his hair, Laine left her comfortable compartment and concentrated her attention on the huge step down to the platform below, the whisper of thought crossing her mind to wonder how the elderly and infirm managed to cope with the distance from train to platform.

A firm hand coming to her arm to assist her gave her the answer that there was always someone there to help. Though when she was safely making it to the platform and she went to offer a 'Grazie' to the railway official; so as that hand on her arm still held firm and she turned, Laine came the nearest ever to passing out cold from sheer and utter shock.

'Zare!' she choked, and was never more in need of his firm supportive hand on her arm.

CHAPTER NINE

STILL not sure that she was not going to faint, Laine was a mass of half-finished sentences. How had he known that . . . How had he got . . . What was . . . And still not believing it, the only sentence she managed to bring out was: 'What are you doing here?'

'Phrased slightly differently, that was my question,' Zare replied, toughness in his voice, toughness in the look of him, an immovable light in his eyes as he refused to let go the hold he still had on her arm.

Her brain in a whirl, it was that toughness in him, that immovable look of him, that dispelled some of her shock. Comprehension started to dawn that either he had been on the same train, or that he had driven like the wind to get there to meet the Florence train. Though how he knew she would be on a train at all was beyond her.

'You—have business in Florence?' she questioned, sufficient wit returning for her to try and bluff it out— just in case this meeting was coincidental.

'I have—business—for want of a better word, with you,' he called her bluff.

'Oh,' she said, stumped for a moment, her heart beating a stacatto beat every other second. 'Well,' she went on, searching desperately for a touch of his arrogance, 'I'm afraid your business will have to be put in writing,' And, trying her hand at surprising him for a change, 'I have a flight booked to England.'

'We have time to discuss our—business, I think,' he replied, not looking surprised at all that she had somehow got a flight ticket which he had not had to pay for, doing a little surprising himself, as he added coldly, 'Your plane doesn't take off until tomorrow afternoon.'

'You *know!*' she gasped. 'How ...' Words failed her.

'Because I phoned several airlines when I knew you didn't intend to return to my home.' Words trembled on her tongue to ask him—when? How had he found out? But, that stiff look still about him, he was saying impatiently, 'We can't talk here. My car is just ...'

'I'm not going anywhere with you,' shot from her in panic before he could finish, it registering as he favoured her with a threatening 'Don't start' look, that since he had his car with him, he must have driven like a demon to get there to meet her train!

Stiffly then, all autocrat, Zare Forturini looked down at her. 'It is not my intention to abduct you, *signorina*—merely to talk, to tell you ...' He broke off, his mouth firming into a straight line at her unyielding look. 'The matter I have to—discuss with you,' he resumed after what she guessed was an Italian count of ten, 'is one I consider to be most private. However, if it is your wish that right here in this railway station I tell you of—certain matters—then ...'

'You'll let me out of the car when—when you've finished telling me of—about these certain matters?' Laine butted in, wary of him still. He would lie his head off if it suited him, she knew that, yet Zare was as proud as she was. And anyway, she excused her weakness, she did not want all and sundry overhearing, if what he had to tell her ended up in them having a blazing row. 'You won't,' she said quickly, 'once you've got me in your car, put your foot down and not stop again until we're back in Valgaro?

For a moment, as he stared at her, he was all arrogance. Then suddenly that arrogance left him. 'I think perhaps by the many times I have—misled— you, I have given you cause to distrust me,' he said quietly. 'But you have my word that once our— discussion is over—if it is your wish,' he added, 'I will personally drive you to Bologna.'

If it was her wish! About to tell him that she was quite capable of taking a train, that while he seemed to think there might be some doubt about her leaving, to her mind, there was no doubt at all; that firm hand had turned her and she could not deny a feeling of pride when walking beside him, his hand still holding her arm, as they went down the platform.

But he was to panic her when, after he had settled her in his car, she expected him to begin to tell her some of his reasons for going from Valgaro to Siena and from there chasing all the way from Siena to Florence after her, he did no more than insert the key in the ignition and started up the car.

'Stop . . .!'

'Try to trust me,' he overrode her. 'I am parked in a restricted zone.'

Laine did her best to try and trust him, but her eyes were alert for road signs that pointed to Siena, until Zare drove into the car park of a hotel.

But she was wary of him still when, coming round to help her out, he informed her that they would talk inside. And she was more wary of him than ever when, known at the hotel, apparently, he collected a key from the desk and guided her towards the lift.

Her feet cemented to the ground as they waited for the lift to arrive, any panic she felt that Zare thought he was taking her up to some hotel bedroom which he obviously kept permanently booked was banished by a feeling of disappointment in him. But she was to discover that her disappointment in him was not necessary, for as the lift doors opened and she refused to budge, he quietly took hold of her arm, but did not propel her forward until he had said:

'I thought we would be more private if I took you to the suite of rooms we reserve for any visiting Italian or overseas business associates.'

Oh, Zare, Laine thought, getting into the lift with him, ashamed of the thoughts she'd had about him, even as she tried to find some of the aggression instinct had been telling her she might be needing ever since he had put the suggestion 'if it is your wish' in relation to her wanting to go to Bologna and the airport.

He had been telling the truth about it being a suite of rooms, she saw the moment he unlocked a door that led into a comfortably furnished sitting room, a small bar standing in the corner for the use of any business man who felt in the need of a reviver after a full day's conference.

'You would care to be seated, Laine?' he asked politely once the door had been closed.

'Thank you,' she murmured, going over to one of the well padded chairs, expecting that he would most likely take the one facing her so that whatever it was he had to discuss with her, which she had to own had her imagination stymied, could begin.

But Zare did not take the chair opposite, nor did he begin to tell her anything. And as her nerves stretched because she had thought never to see him again, but could not deny she was glad to see him, to her mind he never looked like telling her anything.

'Would you like a drink?' was what he did say when he did open his mouth.

He was halfway to the bar before her, 'No, thank you,' reached him. He's nervous about something, flipped into Laine's head, and she knew that she was being an idiot to think such a thing of the strong, always-on-top man who came to stand in front of her to enquire:

'Some other form of refreshment perhaps—coffee?'

She shook her head, knowing that it was not him who was nervous, but her. 'No, thank you,' she said again, her voice growing huskier. 'You said you had something you wanted to say—to discuss with me,' she reminded him, her nerves starting to get so shot that she wanted it done with so that she could get out of there and try to get herself back together again, the way she had done on the train.

'That is true,' he agreed. But again he did not take the chair facing her, but presented her with his back when he took a step away before, as if he had suddenly made up his mind, he turned abruptly, and just as abruptly he rapped:

'I need to know—what is it you feel for my brother? What does he feel for you?'

So that was it! Cristo again! Heat rising at his tone, having been able to see none of his reason for wanting this discussion, Laine saw she must have been blind not to see that, loving his brother as he did, all that Zare was concerned about was his brother's happiness and welfare.

'Surely you're not saying that you've chased after me to tell me at this late stage that you intend to consent to my marrying Cristo after all?' she returned smartly.

'That is precisely what I am *not* saying,' he said sharply, the best he could do, she saw, in keeping a lid on his own aggression.

'Then why the interest in what Cristo and I feel for each other?' she questioned, adding mockingly before he could answer, 'Surely, Zare, you're not going to try to buy me off?' And, her tone growing heated again that that *could* be what all this was about, 'Don't you *dare* offer me money not to contact him ag . . .'

'*Dio!*' he exploded, anger he could not hide blasting her eardrums. 'Do you think I don't *know* by now that you aren't interested in money?'

'What about the two thousand pounds I took from Cristo?' she slammed straight back, her aggression, as ever, refusing to back down when assaulted by his. 'Don't tell me you've forgotten *that*!'

That Zare's aggression appeared to vanish at her challenge told Laine that another bluff had not come off.

'If you're referring to the money he requested for Elaine, then I must tell you that I knew on Saturday evening that it was meant as a gift initially for your mother,' he told her, his tones softening.

Not wanting his aggression, but not wanting that the absence of it should weaken hers, Laine had to force herself to go into battle. 'Well, you didn't know until Cristo told you,' she said tartly, remembering the way he had barked at Cristo to take his arms from her, that he wanted to speak to him privately. 'You wouldn't have believed it,' she asserted, knowing it for the truth, 'unless you'd heard it from Cristo's own lips.'

A muscle in his jaw jerked as she threw that at him. But she was to be surprised when, while she was expecting to be lashed by his aggression again, Zare came forward and took the seat opposite her, although he did not look to be any more relaxed sitting than he had been standing, when, as if searching for the right words, he said:

'Try to understand, Laine—never has Cristo lied to me. I have had the keeping of him since he was ten years old. And in that time, through all his stages of development, never—and there were many escapades where a lie would have served to get him out of trouble—has he ever lied to me. Always,' Zare went on, 'he has been truthful, confessing fully his part in pranks that but for fate smiling on him in adolescence could have landed him in the courts.'

Her aggression had been lost as she listened to what he was telling her. She was even on the way to thinking what a wonderful guardian Zare must have been that, however dreadful the misdemeanour—and some of them must have been pretty terrifying if he had just missed going to court by the skin of his teeth—Cristo had been able to confess honestly to his brother; until she came to remember why he was telling her all this—so she should see how completely he could trust Cristo's word.

'So you see,' he went on quietly, 'when at first you told me you had not taken any money from him, I just knew you had to be lying because, of a certainty, one thing I could be sure of—my brother would not lie to me.'

'It—it must have been a-a blow to you when he told you . . .'

'It was not so much that he told me,' Zare broke in, not surprising her that he had cut in—she had grown used to that, but what did surprise her was that he ended, 'but that I asked him to tell me again for whom he wanted that money.'

'You—*asked* him?' she questioned, her eyes going wide. 'But he had already told you it was for me—

Elaine. You—had no reason to doubt his word in the past!'

'In the past . . .' he said, and halted briefly, '. . . I had not had such as you living under my roof.'

'S-such as me?' stammered Laine, warmth touching her cheeks as her heart started to pound. 'You mean that, even though y-you knew me for a liar—my lying to my parents when I cancelled my trip to New Zea . . .'

'You only lied to them to get them to accept a gift of money from you which would ensure them their hearts' desire. A gift of money,' he added, 'which, had Cristo thought about it a little deeper, he would have seen that your parents nor you would never take from him.'

'He told you all about . . .!'

'I insisted on knowing everything there was to know regarding that money,' he replied. 'As I have said, Laine, having you under my roof, I was soon seeing an honesty in you when you lose your temper, a fierce pride in you that resented me offering you money. I was seeing you returning the few *lire* I did manage to give you, as though it was second nature to you not to be in anyone's debt. And notwithstanding my own observations, I was hearing daily from my household staff about what a caring guest you were, making not the smallest demand on them. None of it,' he went on, 'tying up with the you I believed you to be. So, for the first time ever, I found myself questioning, and,' he admitted, 'not liking that I was questioning, a truth my brother had told me.'

'He didn't lie, exactly,' she defended, too quick in Cristo's defence, she saw, as his brow came down to stir pride in her that even now, if she had got it right, having re-thought his opinion of her, he was still objecting that he might have to have her for a sister-in-law. 'It was partly your fault anyway that he avoided telling you that he wanted the money for a married lady. He . . .'

'He has explained all that,' she was chopped off. 'What he has not told me is . . .' Since he had come in swiftly to cut her off, she was surprised that Zare hesitated and seemed to need a moment to gain some control before he went on, '. . . is what his feelings are for you, and what—you feel for him.'

At once her thoughts went to the scene that had followed Zare coming to Cristo's bedroom, anger spurting in her at his enraged assumptions on finding her there. 'Probably he never told you because you never gave him the chance,' she flared—and was sure, when his hands clenched on the arms of his chair, that Zare too was remembering that same scene.

'Perhaps you're right,' he allowed stiffly. But he was not letting go of the subject matter he had brought up, she heard. 'So now I'm asking you—just what goes on between you and my brother?'

That he was back more or less to the first question he had started with, told Laine that his need to know was the reason why he had chased after her. But knowing now that somewhere along the line, although she had never noticed it, his opinion of her had changed, she still had to know that his opinion of her had not gone up so much that he would countenance her marrying his brother, had marriage been in either of their minds.

'Since you are not going to give your consent to my marrying Cristo,' she said at last, getting to her feet, the interview as far as she was concerned over, 'I don't see that it need worry you what we feel for each other.'

Zare coming to block her way to the door had her

eyes going to his face and taking in the stern look there that said while she might think that the interview was over, Zare Forturini thought there was still more to be said.

'But it does worry me,' he said, when woodenly, waiting for him to get out of her way, she just stared at him.

'Tough on you!' she batted his own phrase at him, and wished that she could feel as hard as she sounded. But just being with him, his dark eyes steady on her, was making her weak.

She went to move round him, but got no further than two steps to the side of him, when a strong hand came to grip her arm and set her heart hammering.

Forced to stand still, wanting to be out of there and on her way, Laine would not look at him again. If he had anything more to say to her, then he could say it to the side of her face.

'It is tough, Laine,' he said at last, his voice thick in his throat, that hand tightening on her arm whether he knew it or not, as, some emotion taking him, he said, 'All his life I have protected Cristo, for he has a soft heart which makes him most vulnerable. But if it is true love this time that he feels—then again I must step in and say that he cannot have the woman he loves.'

Listening to him, Laine could not doubt that it hurt Zare to know that he was going to see to it that the brother he so loved did not have his heart's desire. And for a moment it was a toss-up that she did not there and then tell him that he had no need to be concerned for his brother's happiness, because Cristo was not in love with her. But that was before pride took that moment to take a jab at her, and she was denying that softness of her own heart then, and making her voice hard again, as she replied hostilely:

'Because, despite your changed opinion of me, I'm still not good enough for him, I suppose.'

The rough shake to her arm, even before the exasperated, *'Dio!'* was rapped in her ear, told her that her reply had not pleased him. But as he swung her to face him, she saw aggression breaking in those fierce eyes as angrily, not choosing his words, he nearly floored her by slamming at her, 'The only reason I say that neither he nor anyone else shall have you is that I want you for myself!'

Thunderstruck to hear what had been torn from him in temper, Laine stared, too stupefied for long moments to find her voice to say anything. And when she did find her voice, it was no more than a hoarse croak as she questioned:

'You—want me!'

'You did not know?'

Dumbly, she shook her head. But it was as if by shaking her head she had allowed some intelligence to break through what, so shatteringly, she had just heard.

Oh, what an idiot she was! she thought, looking away from him. Wanting and loving were two entirely different entities. Zare might want her as she wanted him, but by no stretch of the imagination did that mean that he loved her as she loved him!

Aware suddenly that his hand was no longer on her arm, Laine moved a pace or two away, trying to get her thoughts together, as striving for a coolness she was very far from feeling, she said into his general direction:

'I see your dilemma, Zare. You can hardly—have me—and then allow me to become Cristo's wife, can you?'

Pain hit her then, and bit deep. She heard him

move, but shrugged off his hold when his hands came to her shoulders to turn on him viperishly in her hurt that his only worry in taking her to his bed to satiate his desire for her was for Cristo.

'Well, don't lose any more sleep over it,' she blazed, 'I'll obviate the problem for you—you just aren't going to have me!'

'You've got it wrong,' he charged, not a smile about him. 'I didn't mean to have you and then let Cristo . . .'

'I know *that!*' Laine shrieked, her hurt so painful that she wanted to physically lash out at him. 'I'm good enough for one Forturini to bed, aren't I—but not good enough for the other Forturini to marry!'

Suddenly, as though the visible hurt in her was more than he could stand, Zare had moved quickly, and despite her flailing hands as she saw his intention, he had gathered her into his arms.

'Stop it Laine, stop it!' he commanded sternly, his arms securing her to him so she could neither hit him nor get away from him.

Dignity came belatedly. But if to stand quietly within the circle of his arms meant she could then say another word that would not be filled with accusation, that would show him her further hurt. She could not.

But Zare, by the look of it, was not expecting her to say anything. And to have her quiet in the circle of his arms seemed to be what he wanted anyway. For it was after a few seconds of seeing that she had nothing more to shriek at him, that, quietly, he repeated, 'You have it all wrong, *mia cara.*'

Zare calling her his dear made Laine want to hide her face in his shoulder, tears pricking the back of her eyes that so much did she want to be dear to him, but that was not what he wanted.

'You're saying now that you don't want me?' she found voice enough to question.

'You know I want you,' he replied softly. 'Just as I know that you want me.'

That quiet statement brought out an urgent need in her to be free. But Zare was not letting her go; though he did give her enough room to pull back her head to look at him, if she was so minded.

'Do not try to deny it, Laine,' he said to the top of her head. 'Something happens inside you when I kiss you which you cannot help, which I,' he confessed, 'cannot help happening to me too.'

'So——' she said chokily—useless, she saw, to deny anything, 'we're talking about—about desire—and . . . and it—upsetting you that Cristo might be hurt . . .' the edge of temper was coming to her again, and she was glad of it, for wrapped in Zare's arms like this she had been afraid she would give in to anything he asked of her, '. . . that he stands no chance of making me Signora Forturini.'

'I cannot stand by and see my brother give you his name,' he replied, to have her struggle to be free as pride spurted again. Though she stayed motionless in his arms, when he added, pride in him too, pride in the way he said it, 'Just as I cannot stand at all the thought of not having your permission to give you—*my* name.'

The shock of that amazing statement was to fill Laine with so much electrified energy that it would have taken more than Zare's by then not so tight hold on her, to keep her in his arms.

Shaken rigid, she reacted violently. In a flash she was out of his arms, and going round to the other side of a chair, not wanting to be again weakened by his hold.

'Would you mind—very much—repeating that— th—the last part?' she asked jerkily.

He had no objection, it seemed, for his eyes were watching her closely, as he complied quietly, 'I asked you if you would consent to be my wife.'

'I—thought—you did,' said Laine slowly while she waited for her brain to catch up, not trusting him an inch whatever tack he was on.

'Is there any chance,' said Zare, his eyes not leaving hers as he tried to read what was going on in her head, 'that I might have your answer?' And doing nothing for the riot that was going on inside her, he smiled that smile that threatened to finish her, as he said, 'I confess that your agreement to marry me would give me a—great deal of pleasure.'

'I'll bet it would!' Feeling safe behind the chair, no intention in her of coming out from behind it, she saw his smile leave and that scowl she was more familiar with replace it.

'What the devil do you mean by that?' he rapped.

'You must think I came down with the last shower!' she snapped, feeling sick inside that, even if she had even been able to imagine Zare proposing marriage to her, she would never have seen it like this. 'You think that if I say yes to you, then you'll know that Cristo hasn't proposed to me. From that you'll know that he doesn't love me—and from there,' she raced on to tell him the poor best her brain could come up with, 'your conscience clear about him, you think you'll get me into bed with you—then, when the—the lust in you is satisfied, you'll tell me you never meant to marry me in the first place!'

The Italian epithet that left him, was not at all complimentary to her and she was sure that her intelligence had seen right through him. But having for the moment run out of steam, Laine saw his face darken just before he remembered to speak English, when, bluntly, angered at her charge, he told her:

'I could get you into bed any time I want without trouble, but it is not—*lust*—which I am talking of. I . . .'

'Not much you aren't!' Laine jumped in, having had a moment in which to build up another full head of steam. 'You have lied to me from the first—you think I'm going to start believing you *now*, when I *know* what a liar you are?'

That stopped him in his tracks, she saw, but not for long, as he owned, 'I have—lied to you. But . . .'

'Big of you to admit it!' Laine snapped, not surprised she felt out of gear, had she any belief in his proposal she would have tripped over her tongue to say yes. As it was, she was feeling let down again, disappointed in him again even as she had to own that her disappointment in him before had been unwarranted.

'But,' he went on, risking more of her scorn, 'those lies to you became harder and harder the more I knew of you.'

'They would,' she said sarcastically, 'when everyone knows how much you value the truth.' And, remembering, 'You didn't like it when you found out about the fibs I told, did you?'

'The lies you told were necessary,' he replied. Making her blink her disbelief when he added, 'Just as I found my lies to you were necessary.'

'I'm growing more and more intrigued by the minute,' she said waspishly, and saw that he was not liking her attitude one tiny bit. Though, surprisingly, instead of that aggression she knew so well coming to take a flying tackle at hers, stern-faced though he was,

Zare remained calm, his voice having nothing of the roar she wouldn't have been surprised to hear about it, as he said:

'If you will be good enough to hear me out without any more of your sarcastic interruptions, I will do my best to explain to you why I found it necessary to lie to you at all.'

'This,' said Laine, 'I can't wait to hear.'

'You would care to be seated?' he enquired before he got started.

'We've been through that bit,' she countered tartly, staying just where she was.

'Very well,' said Zare, a glint appearing in his eyes that gave her the suspicion he would rather throttle her than tell her anything. Which again caused her some surprise that he intended explaining anything, as he said, 'I will be as brief as possible . . .'

'Don't leave anything out on my account,' she threw in acidly, something else she saw might have him throwing the towel in there and then. But no, doggedly he began.

'It begins with that evening I telephoned you from the hospital when Cristo was out of his head calling for you.'

Her brow wrinkling, Laine put her aggression to one side to ask, puzzled, 'But that wasn't a lie—was it?' remembering Cristo's letter referring to her being the only one, in his fever-racked mind, who could bring his easing cough syrup.

'No—at that time, apart from occasions when no harm is done to prevaricate rather than hurt someone's feelings, I had no use for untruths.'

'So—what changed you?' she asked, unable to hold back on sarcasm as he had asked of her.

'You did,' he replied bluntly. And seeing that his

reply had taken the wind of sarcasm from her sails for a shaken moment of two, he went on quickly, 'I had spoken with you on the telephone. Thrown down that telephone with murder in my heart that you were so uncaring of my brother's life when you could not be bothered to hop on a plane when his need to have you by his bedside was so urgent.'

'I couldn't come—I was broke,' Laine admitted in a rush of self-defence, all sarcasm suddenly gone.

'I know that now,' he said, his severe manner letting up a little. 'But at the time I thought you recently in receipt of his two thousand pounds. However, having put down the phone on you, I was to find, as through the long hours of that night I sat by Cristo's bed, that I could not get your voice out from my ears.'

'I—suppose that was understandable in the circumstances,' Laine found herself letting up a little too, when she hadn't meant to budge an inch.

'That is what I told myself. But, as my brother started to improve, each day seeing a lessening of a need for anxiety, still your voice haunted me. Time and again that huskiness would break uninvited into whatever I was concentrating on, until in the end it became a positive plague. It was then that I knew I would have to see you, confident as I was then that once I had seen the heartless female I then thought you, I could then get on with some work.'

Surprise at what he had just said left her for the moment, not thinking at all. 'You—er—decided to come to see me while you were over in England on business?'

He shook his head. 'I came only to see you,' he answered. 'Only to exorcise you from my mind.'

Again ready to believe him, Laine started to

understand. 'That's why you told me Cristo was not making any progress in his recovery was it?' she asked, her disbelief evident, causing Zare's lips to firm as she added, 'Having exorcised me from your mind, you decided it might be rather—fun—to string me along for a while?'

It looked for a moment as though Zare was going to get angry, for clearly he was not liking her attitude. But, again Laine was to see as he swallowed down his ire, that by the look of it, he was going to take all she threw until he *did* have her believing him. Did *he*, she thought mutinously, have a long wait!

'That is the whole point,' he said, his look level at hers. 'I did not exorcise you from my mind. My purpose in coming to see you was two-fold—to get your voice from my head, and, so I told myself, to give you a piece of my mind by telling you exactly what I thought of you. But,' he went on before she could break in, 'against my will,' he admitted, 'on sight, I found you had a lure for me.'

That, in Laine's view as she recalled that he had not been at all pleasant to her on the visit, was the best lie to date. 'It showed,' she said sourly.

'It was in order that you should not see that attraction I felt that I began on the downward path of—invention,' he told her firmly.

'I knew I'd get the blame for it all,' muttered Laine. But her sarcasm was dying. Even though she faced squarely that she was being led further and further up the garden path, she wanted to hear more. 'When exactly did the lies start?' she found herself asking—and not having to wait for a reply.

'It was just after I had told you that Cristo was out of hospital,' he answered promptly. 'You smiled a beautiful smile that had me for the first time in my life feeling jealous of my brother.'

'Jealous!' Her eyes shot wide. But they were to go wider when, simply, Zare told her:

'That jealousy was mild compared with the jealousy that raged through me when I found you in his bedroom on Sunday. I wanted to kill you both—I believe I might have attempted it had you not obeyed and left his room when you did.'

As she remembered the storming rage Zare had been in, her heart suddenly started a chaotic beating. There had been no untruth in that rage. His fury had been very real—she could still feel it.

'Y-you were—saying,' she prompted, unable just then to cope with what he could or could not be meaning, 'about,' she licked suddenly dry lips, 'about you starting down the road of invention th-that night in England.'

For a second or two, seeing her shock at what he had just revealed, Zare looked as though he might come over to her and take it from there. Then, as if seeing that he owed her more than one explanation, he stayed where he was.

'You smiled,' he resumed, 'and I knew then that since I had heavy business commitments and did not know when I would get the chance to come back to England again, I could not leave you behind.'

Ready to drop at his statement, be it the truth or that he was feeding her a fresh load of lies, Laine swallowed. 'Go on,' she said.

'I was not liking very much this—attraction—I felt for you,' he confessed. 'And liking even less that I found myself saying my brother was not making a good recovery when he was progressing beyond expectations. But, having gone in at the deep end, I was then saying that he had described you to me when he had not, and becoming more and more drawn to you the longer I stayed in your home.'

Not knowing what to believe any longer, she stared unspeaking at him. Everything he was now saying seemed to fit. But she had believed him before!

'Believe me, Laine,' he urged. 'Believe that with you in my home, that attraction I felt for you increasing instead of dwindling as I was sure it would, each lie became more and more difficult to tell.'

'Why?' she asked, her sarcasm beaten by her *wanting* to believe. 'Because you're basically an honest man?'

'That,' he agreed, 'but more because you, above all people, I was finding I did not wish to lie to.'

'Obligatory, was it?' she asked a shade churlishly.

'At the time I thought so,' he replied without hesitation. 'I was not liking at all your eagerness to go and visit Cristo in hospital. Jealousy pure and simple about that made me angry with you on more than one occasion. Jealousy was there to gnaw at me after the morning you had spent in Siena. I had kissed you that night, was sure you felt receptive to me, then had to endure one hell of a night in being torn in two wondering if you were receptive like that with all men— with my brother.'

Laine remembered that night. They had kissed as friends, but the next morning he had been in a cold unfeeling mood. Could she believe that his cold mood had been because of the jealous, wakeful night he had spent? Suddenly, her heart beats were going erratic, her heart choking her throat. But, no words coming from her, as Zare continued, Laine was to be knocked sideways, when he said:

'There was jealous murder in my heart when, on the

night I could have sworn you felt some of the love for me which I have for you, Cristo arrived and looked like taking you away from me. We had been making love,' he reminded her, 'yet within minutes I was having to watch you look as happy to be in his arms as you had been in mine.'

Pink touching her cheeks as she remembered Zare's lovemaking, be she foolish or not, nothing then could make Laine hold back on the, 'You have a—a little—l-love—for me?' that left her tremulous lips.

It was her breath-held look that brought the suggestion of a smile to touch his mouth. 'Do you think I would have kept patience to tell you all I have if I had not?' he asked softly—and had her legs threatening not to hold her when, looking into her eyes, he added, 'Do you think I would have chased after you like one demented when I knew you were not coming back to my home, had I not loved you with my whole heart?'

'Oh, Zare!' moaned Laine, her turn to be torn in two, because she did not know what to believe any more.

But Zare had missed nothing of the expressions that had crossed her face, and in the next instant he had come round to the side of the chair where she was standing. Gently then his two hands came to cup her face, his dark eyes making her look at him, as he said tenderly:

'Believe that if nothing else, *amore mia*. I love you with every part of my being.'

Her eyes just could not doubt the sincerity in his eyes, for steadfastly they refused to look away. But, while warmth and joy surged up in her, Laine had no words to answer him; to say that 'yes', that she believed him.

'I will make you believe it, my Laine,' he promised, as urgently he went on. 'If you love me just a little, then marry me, and I will spend the rest of my life making you see how it has been with me since that day I took you into Siena when you smiled at me with that look of fairy tale enchantment on your face.'

At those words, a deep huskiness in her voice, at last Laine found vocal release. 'I . . . I feel—more than a little enchanted—right at this moment,' she said shyly, but had to tell him, 'It seems unbelievable that you love me. Oh, Zare,' she begged, 'tell me again, so I can believe it.'

'You love me—just a little?' he asked, his eyes pleading with her to tell him that she did.

She gave him a shy smile, and found courage then to tell him, 'Why else do you think I ran away?'

With an exultant cry, Zare had her in his arms. And Laine had her heart's desire, telling her how desperately he loved her, Zare was making her believe it. Gathering her in his arms, he kissed her reverently, those arms tightening possessively as he kissed every part of her face.

'How can you love me when I have been such a disagreeable, lying brute to you?' he murmured. And he was raining kisses on her face again as he threatened, 'But don't you dare love anyone else— ever!'

In a world which she had never thought to be hers, Laine had not the slightest objection to make when Zare picked her up in his arms and took her to sit with him in one of the armchairs.

It was there, in close harmony, his words of love thrilling her as again he told her of his love, that in between kisses Zare confessed that she had already begun to ensnare him on that drive from the airport to

Valgaro. She was delighted to hear how, always before in a hurry to get home, that while telling himself it was just her hostility he found stimulating, that later he had had to admit that it was from pure enjoyment of having her so close to him that he had not put his foot down on that drive.

Again they kissed, until Zare broke the kiss, still jealous as he asked about the boy-friend she had left behind in England. But her confession about Austin brought her not a hard-eyed look for the way she had used him, but a relieved look and a lengthening kiss that left her breathless.

Zare's caresses were to send her as mindless as they had before. But suddenly he was taking his hand from the smooth silky skin inside her dress, a groan leaving him as he tidied her clothing.

'Oh, how I wish you had not accused me of asking you to marry me only so that I could get you to agree to go to bed with me!' And while, totally enraptured, Laine would have had no objection to make to any suggestion he made, he told her ruefully, a proof of his love there if she needed it, 'Now I shall just have to wait for you until we *are* married.'

Transported, Laine didn't think she wanted to wait very long. Though her question was tentative as she asked, 'Could we ... That is—could I suggest, that we—er—um—don't have a very long engagement?'

Zare raising one eyebrow teasingly aloft had her nervously wondering if she had been too forward. But in no time he was making her chuckle.

'You, my heart, have taken the words right out of my mouth,' he told her. 'But first we have a lot to accomplish.'

'We have?' she questioned. And watching him, she saw his humour depart, his face all at once serious.

'The first thing I must do is to visit Milan to tell Cristo personally that much as I love him and would spare him pain if I could, my love for you outweighs all others.'

'I don't think he'll be very upset,' Laine told him quickly.

'He is in love with you, *cara*.'

In a rush, she said, 'He may love me as a sister, but he's not in love with me.' The next moment she was off Zare's lap going in search of her handbag, explaining as she went. 'It wasn't Cristo vowing his love for me when you came in and saw me in his bedroom yesterday, when—when he was about to kiss me—if that's what you thought.' She wasn't surprised that what she was telling him came out sounding rather muddled, though Zare, she thought, had got the gist of what she was trying to say as, her shoulder-bag run to earth, she returned to her happy haven on his lap.

'It wasn't?'

Laine shook her head, passing him Cristo's letter. 'Your brother became part of my family, Zare—I think you'll see from what he's written that a sister is how he regards me.' Giving him a moment to read, she saw relief start to flood his face. 'Cristo was getting ready to shower when I went to his room,' she went on explaining. 'But I only went to his room to ask him to lend me my air fare. He was only going to kiss me because he knew how unhappy I was.'

Cristo's letter read, a smile that was wonderful for her to see left Zare. 'I shall see to it that you have few unhappy moments in the future,' he vowed then, and pulled her back against him to bestow a warm kiss to her mouth. But as if remembering his vow not to touch her until they were man and wife, he was pulling back to tell her, 'I knew Cristo had supplied your air fare when Anna-Maria confessed to me about the bulky envelope she had left in your room.'

'Anna-Maria confessed?' Laine repeated, guessing there was more than that to it. But she heard that she hadn't known the half of it when Zare told her how, having suspected she was up to something, he had decided not to go to work that day, and how he had been in his study when Angelina had come to tell him that Giuseppe had just returned from an errand that should have taken him five minutes, and how he had excused his being late in bringing back the article she had been waiting for, by telling her that when signorina Laine had jumped up beside him and told him to take her to Siena, he had not liked to refuse.

'He wasn't going to Siena!'

Zare's grin was freely there at her astonishment. Though that grin faded as he told her, 'Angelina's one worry was how you would get back home—my one worry was that you did not intend to come home at all. I chased up to your room, saw that while you were gone, your clothes were there, and for the briefest moment I was ready to breathe easier again. That was before my eyes went to where only the day before I had seen the plate you love so much. The dressing table was bare—I knew then that you did not intend coming back.'

'I couldn't leave it behind—it reminds me of your home.'

'The forsythia?'

'You knew all the time?'

'I was hoping it meant what I thought it meant. Hoping that if you did not hate my home then you wanted a reminder of it, that maybe you did not hate me as much as I deserve your hate.'

'Oh, Zare,' Laine said softly. 'I tried to hate you, but I couldn't.'

Unable to stop himself, Zare kissed her again before he told her, 'Your look of enchantment with *il Campo* will stay with me for ever. It was the memory of that look that made me certain you would not be able to resist one last look when Giuseppe told me he had dropped you off near there.'

'Was that where you went first?'

Zare nodded, and held her tightly as though to say she must never run away and give him a fright like that ever again.

'I should have asked you to marry me yesterday as I intended,' he said. 'It would have . . .'

'You were going to propose yesterday!'

'That was part of the reason I was as mad as hell when I came home and found you with Cristo,' he owned. 'I'd spent the day away from you purposely to try and get things into perspective.'

'Having sent Cristo to Florence,' she inserted, and received his wonderful unashamed grin again.

'And returned home,' he resumed, 'with the thought that my brother would just have to be hurt, that I could not stand seeing him with his arms around you again. But the first thing I saw when I came back was his car, to tell me, when I was positive my aunt and uncle would insist he stayed to dinner, that he had returned before me. I was still hoping to have a favourable hearing when I went to your room. Your door stood open, and I felt black jealousy so that, even not believing it could be so, I went along to Cristo's room—I could have murdered the pair of you!'

'You did—er—look a shade angry,' Laine commented happily—and was kissed very thoroughly for her sauce. Until, determinedly, Zare suddenly set her to her feet.

'We have a lot to do,' he growled, delighting her as she heard that thick note in his voice. 'I think, for my sanity, we had better get started.'

'We're going to Milan to tell Cristo?' she guessed.

Zare shook his head. 'I can tell him what I have to over the phone now,' he smiled. 'More urgently, I have to check round to see if we can take in Australia as part of our honeymoon, or if we have to make Australia a short visit, and marry when we get back.'

'We're going to *Australia*!' Laine squeaked.

'Don't you want to see your brother married?' he asked tenderly, his eyes full of the love he had for her.

'Oh, Zare Forturini,' said Laine, tears in her eyes, 'is it any wonder that I love you.'

'In a word,' he said softly, his arms coming out to hold her, 'yes. But,' he added, 'never, never stop.'

HARLEQUIN
PREMIERE AUTHOR EDITIONS

6 EXCITING HARLEQUIN AUTHORS
—6 OF THEIR BEST BOOKS!

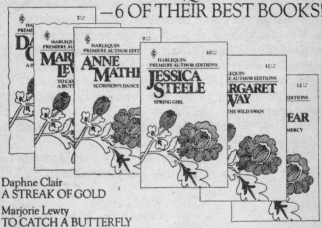

Daphne Clair
A STREAK OF GOLD

Marjorie Lewty
TO CATCH A BUTTERFLY

Anne Mather
SCORPIONS' DANCE

Jessica Steele
SPRING GIRL

Margaret Way
THE WILD SWAN

Violet Winspear
DESIRE HAS NO MERCY

Harlequin is pleased to offer these six very special titles, out of print since 1980. These authors have published over 250 titles between them. Popular demand required that we reissue each of these exciting romances in new beautifully designed covers.

Available in April wherever paperback books are sold, or through Harlequin Reader Service. Simply send your name, address and zip or postal code, with a check or money order for $2.50 for each copy ordered (includes 75¢ for postage and handling) payable to Harlequin Reader Service, to:

Harlequin Reader Service

In the U.S.
P.O. Box 52040
Phoenix, AZ 85072-2040

In Canada
P.O. Box 2800
Postal Station A
5170 Yonge Street
Willowdale, Ontario
M2N 6J3

PAE-1

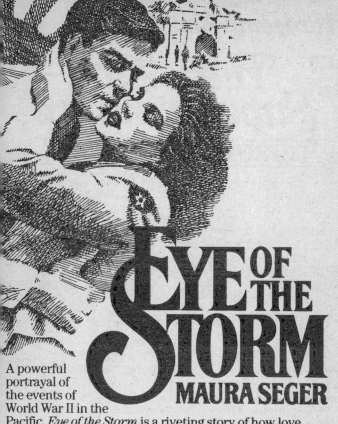

EYE OF THE STORM

MAURA SEGER

A powerful portrayal of the events of World War II in the Pacific, *Eye of the Storm* is a riveting story of how love triumphs over hatred. Aboard a ship steaming toward Corregidor, Army Lt. Maggie Lawrence meets Marine Sgt. Anthony Gargano. Despite military regulations against fraternization, they resolve to face together whatever lies ahead.... A searing novel by the author named by *Romantic Times* as 1984's Most Versatile Romance Author.

Harlequin Announces...

Harlequin Superromance™

IMPROVED EXCELLENCE

NSUP-A-1

Beginning with February releases (titles #150 to #153) each of the four Harlequin Superromances will be 308 pages long and have a regular retail price of $2.75 ($2.95 in Canada).

The new shortened Harlequin Superromance guarantees a faster-paced story filled with the same emotional intensity, character depth and plot complexity you have come to expect from Harlequin Superromance.

The tighter format will heighten drama and excitement, and that, combined with a strong well-written romance, will allow you to become more involved with the story from start to finish.

WATCH FOR A SPECIAL INTRODUCTORY PRICE ON HARLEQUIN SUPERROMANCE TITLES #150-#153 IN FEBRUARY

Available wherever paperback books are sold or through Harlequin Reader Service:

In the U.S.
P.O. Box 52040
Phoenix, AZ 85072-2040

In Canada
P.O. Box 2800, Postal Station A
5170 Yonge Street
Willowdale, Ontario M2N 6J3

Take these
4 best-selling novels
FREE

Yes! Four sophisticated, contemporary love stories by four world-famous authors of romance FREE, as your introduction to the Harlequin Presents subscription plan. Thrill to **Anne Mather**'s passionate story BORN OUT OF LOVE, set in the Caribbean.... Travel to darkest Africa in *Violet Winspear*'s TIME OF THE TEMPTRESS....Let *Charlotte Lamb* take you to the fascinating world of London's Fleet Street in MAN'S WORLD....Discover beautiful Greece in **Sally Wentworth**'s moving romance SAY HELLO TO YESTERDAY.

 *The very finest in romance fiction*

Join the millions of avid Harlequin readers all over the world who delight in the magic of a really exciting novel. EIGHT great NEW titles published EACH MONTH! Each month you will get to know exciting, interesting, true-to-life people .... You'll be swept to distant lands you've dreamed of visiting .... Intrigue, adventure, romance, and the destiny of many lives will thrill you through each Harlequin Presents novel.

Get all the latest books before they're sold out!
As a Harlequin subscriber you actually receive your personal copies of the latest Presents novels immediately after they come off the press, so you're sure of getting all 8 each month.

Cancel your subscription whenever you wish!
You don't have to buy any minimum number of books. Whenever you decide to stop your subscription just let us know and we'll cancel all further shipments.